From the BookFest 2026 3rd Place–Winning Romance Series

She Came at the Glass Heel
Book 2

Room 312

Tatiana Vixen Reyes

For Collette—my beta reader, my biggest fan, and my friend. None of this would have been possible without her.

Chapter 1

Arrival at The Heel's Nest

Lena ducked through the unmarked door, escaping Chicago's January fury that had left her neck raw and stinging. The lobby's sudden hush felt like a physical embrace after the wind's relentless screaming. She tapped her boots against the entry mat—some designer brand, no doubt—making sure no betraying slush marred the immaculate marble floor. The Glass Heel maintained two separate entrances: the main one leading directly to the club, while this side door remained intentionally discreet, distinguished only by a modest brass plaque that barely separated it from the anonymous West Side storefronts flanking it.

The lobby was surprisingly intimate for a venue boasting The Heel's prestigious reputation. Just inside the entrance stood a sleek reception desk fashioned from rich, dark wood, its surface polished to a mirror-like sheen. Three mid-century chairs, each an elegant nod to minimalist design, were thoughtfully arranged around a low table. This table was meticulously stacked with art books, their spines a spectrum of color and design, inviting guests to explore their glossy pages. The walls were adorned with an array of local photography, each piece capturing the essence of the surrounding area with striking clarity.

Lena, with the practiced eye of someone whose profession demanded acute attention to detail, brushing off her coat and began to take in her surroundings. The air was infused with the subtle, earthy aroma of sandalwood, a scent so delicate it seemed to whisper rather than announce itself. The acoustics of the room were such that sound was absorbed into the space, creating a tranquil hush rather than a cacophony of echoes. Atop the reception desk sat a small vase, its presence understated yet luxurious, holding a bouquet of peonies. These flowers, out of season and undoubtedly costly, added a touch of opulence to the room, their soft petals a contrast to the sleek, modern lines of the furniture. The entire space could fit in her Milwaukee apartment twice over, yet it exuded a sophistication and elegance that expanded its dimensions beyond mere physical size.

A single elevator stood at the back wall, its doors a burnished gold with "The Heel's Nest" etched in flowing script. This was the real entrance then—the threshold between the outside world and whatever waited above. She'd read about the club on the street level, of course, had seen the carefully curated Instagram posts and breathless write-ups in competing travel magazines. But the hotel itself above the club remained something of a mystery, mentioned in whispers among her queer travel writer colleagues.

Perfect for new month's *Queer Compass*'s "Hidden Gems" feature.

Lena shifted her trusty leather satchel, the worn cognac hide creaking against her hip as she adjusted its weight. The familiar heft of her Canon EOS R5 nestled inside brought a quiet confidence—its presence as reassuring as an old friend's hand on her shoulder. This bag, with its constellation of scuffs from Barcelona's cobblestones and that coffee spill in Kyoto, had weathered fourteen countries across four continents. The brass buckle, polished to a honey glow from years of anxious thumbing, caught the lobby's subtle lighting. Three days in this enigmatic hotel meant seventy-two hours of potential shots—the kind of intimate, impossible-to-stage moments that made her editor at *Queer Compass* practically purr with satisfaction.

The soft ding of the elevator drew her attention, but before she could step toward it, a man emerged from what had appeared to be merely a shadow in the paneling—a door so seamlessly integrated into the dark wood behind the reception desk that its outline was visible only when it swung open. The hidden entrance revealed itself with a whisper of well-oiled hinges, as if the building itself were sharing a secret.

"Ms. Marquez?" His voice carried across the small space with practiced ease. "Welcome to The Heel's Nest."

He moved with an effortless grace that matched the space—polished but not pretentious. Six-foot-two at least, with a tailored charcoal suit that hung perfectly from broad shoulders, he navigated the intimate lobby like a dancer familiar with every inch of his stage. His warm brown eyes—the color of bourbon held up to firelight—crinkled slightly at the corners when he smiled, which he was doing now as he extended a hand adorned with a single silver signet ring that caught the subtle overhead lighting.

"Adrian Vega, concierge. We've been expecting you."

Lena shook his hand, noting the firm grip and the way he held eye contact just long enough to feel personal without becoming uncomfortable.

"Your timing is impeccable," he said, moving behind the desk and tapping at a tablet. "Another hour and you might have been redirected to O'Hare for the night. This storm isn't playing around."

"Lucky me," Lena said, slipping off her gloves and tucking them into her coat pocket. "I'm guessing you don't get many walk-ins with this entrance being so... subtle."

Adrian laughed. "That's by design. The club gets the spotlight while we offer the sanctuary." He looked up from the tablet. "*Queer Compass*, right? I'm a subscriber. Your piece on those hidden lesbian beaches in Portugal was brilliant."

A small flush of pride warmed Lena's cheeks. "Always nice to meet a reader."

"Room 312 should be perfect for you," Adrian said. "Third level, east side. It has the perfect snow view—though tonight it might be more of a blizzard theater."

He came around the desk again. "Let me show you up. Your luggage arrived earlier—we've already placed it in your room."

The elevator doors parted soundlessly at his light touch, revealing an interior bathed in opulence. The gold theme extended within, with polished brass panels gleaming softly under the subtle, ambient lighting. This gentle illumination enveloped the space, casting a warm, golden glow over Adrian's features as he reached out and pressed the button for the third floor. The atmosphere was one of refined elegance, with every detail meticulously designed to create a sense of luxury and comfort.

"The club entrance is accessible from the second floor of the Nest," he explained as they ascended. "Though with this weather, you might want to stay in tonight. Room service is available until 2 AM, and the minibar is complimentary for press."

The elevator hummed softly beneath their feet, a gentle vibration that echoed through the enclosed space. Lena watched intently as the floor numbers lit up one by one: L, 2, 3. Each number flickered to life in a warm, amber glow against the polished metal panel, marking their ascent through the building. The quiet whir of the machinery accompanied their steady rise, creating a serene, almost rhythmic soundtrack to their journey.

"Each room has its own unique theme," Adrian continued. "Yours is one of my favorites. And if you're interested in the history of the place, Echo's suite is on the fourth floor. She's been with The Heel since the beginning, back when this building was still half-abandoned. She's usually happy to chat with press, if you'd like me to arrange something."

The elevator doors slid open with a gentle chime, unveiling a hallway adorned with textured wallpaper in a rich, deep burgundy hue. The walls were elegantly decorated with framed pictures of women, each portrait capturing a moment frozen in time. As Adrian guided her down the corridor, Lena observed the quaint charm of the setting. Instead of the sleek, impersonal modern key cards she was accustomed to, Adrian reached into his pocket and retrieved an actual brass key, its golden surface gleaming softly under the corridor's warm lighting.

"We're a bit old-fashioned in some ways," he said, catching her glance. "Echo believes there's something more... intimate about using a real key. Each one is unique to its room."

He paused in front of a door labeled 312, where an ornate brass plate gleamed, engraved with the words "The Muse's Retreat" just below the numbers. The key, cool and smooth in his hand, slid effortlessly into the lock, producing a satisfying click that echoed softly in the hallway.

"Here we are," Adrian said, pushing the door open and stepping aside. "Your home for the next few days."

Lena stepped inside, and a gasp escaped her lips as her eyes widened in sheer awe. The room unfolded before her like a masterpiece, a harmonious blend of cozy intimacy and expansive grandeur that took her breath away. Majestic floor-to-ceiling windows stretched high, framing an enchanting scene outside where delicate snowflakes whirled and twirled in a mesmerizing dance, piling up in soft, thick layers on the frozen ground, creating a serene winter wonderland. Yet inside, an inviting warmth wrapped around her like a cherished embrace. The walls and furnishings were a captivating eclectic mix of bold patterns, each surface a vibrant feast for the eyes, bursting with color and texture. Hanging from the walls were a few framed pieces of sensual queer art, their vivid imagery captivating and thought-provoking. Plush fabrics draped luxuriously over cushions and armchairs, inviting one to sink into their comforting embrace, promising relaxation and tranquility. Ambient lighting bathed the room gently, glowing softly as if emanating from an unseen source, casting a gentle, golden hue that wrapped around the room like a tender embrace, infusing the space with a sense of peace and serenity.

"This is... not what I expected," she admitted, her eyes sweeping over the room. The mahogany writing desk was positioned with precision before the large bay window, allowing early evening light to flood the leather-inlaid surface, highlighting the intricate Art Nouveau carvings of women's faces that adorned each drawer pull. Nearby, a crimson velvet chaise lounge beckoned invitingly, draped with hand-woven Peruvian alpaca throws in jewel tones of sapphire, emerald, and amethyst that whispered of warmth and comfort against the winter chill. Dominating the room was a grand king-sized bed, its wrought-iron frame crowned with a canopy of sheer, gossamer silk that fluttered softly with the slightest breeze from the hidden vents, adding an ethereal touch to the sanctuary-like space. Half-concealed in the shadow of a potted palm near the bed was a discreet rosewood chest, its brass lock gleaming in the low light, hinting at secrets contained within.

"The Muse's Retreat is designed for creative souls," Adrian explained, handing her the key. "Each room tells a different story. Some guests return specifically for their favorite themes."

Her luggage, with its well-worn leather exterior and brass clasps, sat neatly beside an antique wardrobe, its dark wood polished to a gleaming finish. The wardrobe's ornate carvings and intricate details whispered of a bygone era. On the writing desk, a leather-bound journal lay open, its pages slightly yellowed and inviting, resting beside a sleek fountain pen, its silver nib poised and ready to capture thoughts and musings.

"For your thoughts," Adrian said, following her gaze. "Though I suppose these days most writers prefer laptops."

"Sometimes the old ways have their charm," Lena replied, running her fingers over the cream-colored pages.

"I'll leave you to settle in. The room service menu is by the bed. If you need anything at all..." He handed her a business card with his name and a direct number. "Day or night."

Once he departed, Lena let the door close softly behind him and shrugged off her coat, feeling the fabric slide from her shoulders. She inhaled deeply, the air tinged with the delicate scent of jasmine intertwined with the earthy aroma of cedar, a subtle blend that seemed to linger in the room like a gentle embrace. She carefully unpacked her camera first—her most cherished tool, as always—cradling it like a precious artifact. Next, she extracted her laptop from its snug compartment, ready to begin the meticulous task of documenting the space around her. Her eyes roamed over the collection of art books, meticulously arranged by color, creating a vibrant spectrum that lined the shelves. The lighting in the room was soft and warm, casting a gentle glow that seemed to make her skin shimmer as if lit from within, a luminescence that added an ethereal quality to the serene ambiance.

She pressed her hand against the mattress, feeling its perfect blend of firmness and softness, like a gentle embrace that promised comfort. With a quick motion, she captured a picture of the view beyond the window: the Chicago skyline, once a sharp silhouette, now shrouded and softened by the swirling, thickening snowflakes that danced through the air. The windows, crafted with impressive insulation, created a silent barrier; she could witness the storm's fury but was cocooned in silence, the outside world muted and distant.

She carefully angled her camera to capture the intricate play of light cascading across the opulent velvet headboard, its rich texture absorbing and reflecting the soft glow. Next, she moved to photograph the bathroom, a true marvel of vintage luxury and elegance. Dominating the space was a magnificent clawfoot tub, spacious enough to comfortably accommodate two, its porcelain surface gleaming pristinely. The marble countertops exuded timeless sophistication, their smooth, cool surface a perfect complement to the room's aesthetic. Brass fixtures, polished to a warm, inviting sheen, gleamed under the soft illumination of artfully placed sconces, casting a cozy ambiance throughout the room. Beside the sink, there was an exquisite collection of toiletries housed in amber glass bottles, each meticulously labeled in the same elegant, flowing script that adorned the door to room 312, adding a touch of refined continuity to the hotel's theme.

Her phone buzzed in her pocket just as she was

capturing the intricate tile work on the floor. A weather alert flashed across her screen: "Blizzard Warning: 10-14 inches expected overnight. Travel not advised."

Lena frowned as she moved back to the window, her gaze fixed on the swirling chaos outside. The snow was falling faster now, with flakes growing larger and more insistent, like tiny white dancers in a chaotic ballet. The weather app displayed a daunting mass of blue and purple sweeping ominously across the radar, casting a foreboding shadow over Chicago. The city seemed to brace itself under the weight of the impending storm, the sky a dark canvas painted with winter's relentless fury.

"So much for exploring the city tonight," she murmured, scrolling through the forecast. The storm would peak around midnight, with winds gusting to forty miles per hour. She'd planned to visit a few neighborhood spots Adrian had mentioned—a queer-owned bookstore and a café known for its community events—but venturing out in this weather seemed foolish at best.

She tapped her rose gold iPhone against her chin, the cool metal a contrast to her flushed skin as she weighed her options. The responsible choice would be to stay put beneath the gossamer canopy, but her looming deadline hung over her like the storm clouds outside. The article needed to capture not just The Heel's Nest's velvet-draped luxury, but how its bohemian pulse connected to the gritty, vibrant community beyond its ornate doors.

Lena studied her reflection in the bathroom's gilt-edged mirror, the soft lighting casting shadows beneath her cheekbones. Her travel outfit—practical indigo jeans and a cashmere sweater the color of winter wheat—wouldn't cut it for The Glass Heel's sophisticated clientele. She unzipped her vintage leather suitcase and rifled through her carefully rolled options, manicured fingers pulling out a sleek black jumpsuit with a plunging neckline she'd packed just in case. She paired it with her only good jewelry—fourteen-karat gold hoops that caught the light when she moved her head and a delicate chain necklace with a tiny crescent moon pendant that nestled in the hollow of her throat.

The transformation was subtle but effective, like a butterfly emerging from its chrysalis. Professional enough to conduct interviews without intimidating subjects, stylish enough to blend into the velvet shadows of a high-end club. She refreshed her lipstick—a warm terracotta that brought out the amber flecks in her hazel eyes—and slipped her digital recorder, laptop, and laminated press credentials into a small crossbody bag of buttery black leather.

With her decision set, her heartbeat accelerated with excitement. The snow-covered neighborhood could wait; tonight she planned to explore the vibrant core of the Heel, where music would pulse through the floor and cocktails would shine like gems under dim lighting. She intended to begin by photographing the corridors of the Nest, gradually making her way to the club, unsure if it would be open given the impending blizzard. If fortune favored her, she might even catch sight of the mysterious Echo that Adrian had mentioned, the performer whose name had been spoken with admiration in every review she'd come across.

Chapter 2

First Sparks in the Nest

The corridor stretched before Lena like a museum dedicated to forgotten history, each portrait on the burgundy walls a window into a life that deserved remembrance. She adjusted her camera's aperture, seeking the perfect balance to capture the gentle glow of the sconces without losing the subtle texture of the wallpaper beneath.

"Let's see what stories you have to tell," she murmured, framing her first shot.

The third-floor hallway of The Heel's Nest stretched one hundred and fifty feet long, its burgundy damask wallpaper catching the amber glow from antique brass sconces. Lena's camera strap dug into her neck as she moved from portrait to portrait, her fingertips hovering centimeters from the ornate gilt frames. Each photograph—some sepia-toned, others hand-colored with fading pigments—captured transgender women with penciled eyebrows, painted lips, and eyes that held stories of midnight raids and back-alley beatings. The brass nameplates beneath, polished to a honeyed sheen, bore engravings of names, alongside dates that measured lives cut short by violence, illness, or the slow poison of societal rejection.

Marsha P. Johnson, 1945-1992. The familiar face looked back at Lena with that radiant smile—lips painted a deep crimson, parted just enough to reveal the gap between her front teeth—that had launched a revolution at Stonewall and beyond. The portrait captured her in profile against a summer sky, wearing a crown of fresh red roses and white daisies intertwined with baby's breath, their petals casting delicate shadows across her dark skin. Her eyes, lined with perfect wings of kohl, sparkled with a defiance and joy that seemed to transcend the gilt frame containing her image.

"Perfect," Lena whispered as she captured the play of light across the frame, the way the sconce above cast a halo effect around Marsha's flower crown.

She moved methodically down the hall, photographing the interplay of shadow and light on each portrait. Sylvia Rivera, 1951-2002—captured mid-speech at a rally, one finger jabbing skyward, her dark hair whipping across angular cheekbones flushed with righteous anger. Christine Jorgensen, 1926-1989—poised in a pencil skirt and cashmere sweater, her blonde coiffure immaculate, the subtle lift of her chin betraying the steel beneath her poise. Their gazes seemed to follow her, silent witnesses to her documentation of this sacred space.

The plush burgundy carpet muffled her footsteps as she worked, the only sounds the soft mechanical click of her camera shutter and her own measured breathing that fogged slightly in the cool, still air. Lena knelt to capture the way the recessed baseboard lighting created dramatic shadows beneath each frame, transforming the corridor into a cathedral of remembrance, each portrait a stained-glass window illuminating forgotten saints.

Once Lena finished photographing the third floor, she descended the grand, curved staircase to the second level, her fingers lightly grazing the smooth, polished banister that glistened under the ambient lighting. Here, the atmosphere transformed subtly yet distinctly. The walls were adorned with portrait photographs, capturing more contemporary faces—women who had graced The Heel's Nest since its founding. In contrast to the memorial wall above, these portraits were accompanied by gleaming brass plaques, each inscribed with names and the dates of their inaugural visits: Laverne Cox, June 6, 2014; Janet Mock, September 16, 2016.

The brass nameplates shone brilliantly under the soft, warm lighting, each one polished to a flawless mirror finish. Lena was captivated by the way the light danced across them, casting golden halos on the richly textured wallpaper that enveloped the room. She took a moment to photograph the elegant, sweeping curve of the stairwell, which gracefully descended toward what Adrian had referred to as the club's private entrance—a grand doorway of dark, lustrous wood adorned with intricate carvings that seemed to whisper promises of secrets and pleasures waiting just beyond.

Through her viewfinder, she framed the junction where the staircase met the second-floor landing, where the wood grain of the banister formed a natural leading line toward a particularly striking portrait of a woman with sharp cheekbones and knowing eyes. The composition was perfect—the warm amber light casting the woman's features in a dreamy glow, as if she'd stepped straight out of a cherished memory.

After capturing several angles of the staircase, Lena moved along the second-floor hallway, methodically documenting each portrait. Unlike the memorial gallery above, these images pulsed with life—women who had found sanctuary within these walls, who had perhaps walked these same corridors where Lena now stood. There was an intimacy to these photographs that the historical portraits lacked, a sense of belonging rather than remembrance.

She paused before a striking black and white portrait of a woman with high cheekbones and eyes that seemed to pierce through the camera lens. The nameplate read: "Carmen Rodriguez, April 15, 2008." The date was just months after The Heel's Nest had opened its doors. Lena wondered about Carmen's story—what had brought her here in those early days, what she had found within these walls.

After she had captured the essence of the second floor with her camera, Lena took the elevator down to the ground level. The golden light spilled into the corners like thick, flowing honey, infusing warmth into the polished wood of the reception desk and casting gentle, waltzing shadows that glided across the smooth concrete floor. Lena carefully adjusted her camera settings to accommodate the softer, lower light, intent on capturing the delicate interplay between the lavishness of the setting and its understated elegance.

She strategically positioned herself near the entrance, angling her camera to frame the reception area with the gleaming elevator doors visible in the background. This composition whispered a story—one of arrival, of anticipation, of the journey from the ordinary world outside to the serene sanctuary above. With each click of the shutter, she captured multiple shots, slightly shifting her stance each time, in pursuit of the perfect balance that would encapsulate the scene's nuanced beauty.

"Finding what you need?"

Lena startled, her fingers fumbling against the

textured grip of her camera as it swung precariously from her neck. Adrian stood framed in the hidden doorway his tall silhouette backlit by the fluorescent glow of what she now recognized as the staff area. Steam curled in lazy arabesques from the two burgundy ceramic mugs clutched in his long-fingered hands, the rich, nutty aroma of freshly ground coffee already reaching her across the room.

"I didn't mean to interrupt your artistic process," he said, his lips curving into that same half-smile she'd noticed earlier. "But I thought you might appreciate some fuel."

"You're a lifesaver," Lena said, lowering her camera. The aroma of freshly brewed coffee reached her, rich and inviting. "I was just finishing up down here."

Adrian handed her one of the mugs—a heavy ceramic piece glazed in midnight blue. "My personal blend," he said with a conspiratorial wink. "Guests never get this—just whatever fancy roast Echo orders for the rooms. Consider it a professional courtesy."

The midnight-blue ceramic mug radiated heat into Lena's palms, its weight substantial and grounding. Steam spiraled upward in translucent ribbons, carrying an intoxicating bouquet that made her eyes flutter closed for a moment. She inhaled deeply, letting the aroma fill her sinuses before taking that first tentative sip.

"This is incredible," she admitted, taking another sip. "I might have to include it in my article."

"The secret coffee blend of The Heel's most notorious concierge," Adrian finished with a self-deprecating chuckle. "Don't worry, I won't make you sign an NDA for the recipe. Though Echo might if she knew I was raiding her premium beans."

Lena cradled the midnight-blue mug between her palms, her fingertips tracing the subtle imperfections in the ceramic glaze as warmth radiated through her chilled hands. The richness of the coffee lingered on her tongue—velvety dark chocolate undertones melding with hints of cardamom and cinnamon that transported her instantly to her abuela's kitchen in Pilsen, where the old woman would stand at the stove on frost-bitten Chicago mornings, wooden molinillo whirring between her palms until the Mexican hot chocolate frothed with tiny perfect bubbles that would cling to Lena's upper lip like a sweet mustache.

"Single origin?" she asked, taking another appreciative sip.

"A blend, actually. Ethiopian Yirgacheffe for the brightness, a touch of Sumatran for body." Adrian leaned against the reception desk, his posture relaxed yet somehow still impeccably professional. "My sister runs a small-batch roastery in Pilsen. She lets me experiment with her beans."

"Talented family," Lena murmured, noticing how the coffee's steam fogged the lens of her camera. She carefully wiped it clean with the microfiber cloth from her pocket.

"Get what you needed?" Adrian nodded toward her camera. "The portraits are a favorite with our guests. Echo started collecting them when she first opened the place. Says they're our guardian angels."

"They're stunning. The lighting up there is perfect for photography." Lena hesitated, then added, "I'd love to know more about the women on the second floor. The contemporary portraits."

Adrian's eyes lit up. "Each one has stayed here at least once. Some are regulars. Echo believes in documenting our history as it happens, not just honoring what came before." He took a sip from his own mug, a burgundy twin to hers. "Speaking of history in the making, I was thinking you might want to check out The Glass Heel tonight."

"In this weather?" Lena glanced toward the entrance,

where snow was now piling against the bottom of the door in a growing white ridge.

"That's the beauty of our setup." Adrian's voice dropped conspiratorially. "The second-level interior entrance means you never have to brave the elements. The door next to Carmen Rodriguez's portrait? That leads straight to the club's VIP section."

Lena felt a flutter of excitement. "Is the club even open with this storm?"

"The Heel never closes," he said with quiet pride. "We've operated through blackouts, protests, and blizzards worse than this. Tonight's signature cocktail is the Winter Solstice—vodka infused with rosemary and black peppercorns, topped with a cranberry foam that melts on your tongue like fresh snow." His description painted such a vivid picture that Lena could almost taste it.

"And the music?" she asked, already mentally calculating which lens would work best in low-light club conditions.

"Tonight's set is by DJ Heather—not the famous one, our own resident talent. She weaves house and trip-hop together like silk threads. When that bass drops, you feel it here," Adrian tapped two fingers against his sternum as he set his empty mug on the desk with his other hand. "Weeknights bring a different crowd. More discerning. Less transient. The regulars who've seen things, done things. People whose secrets you'd want to know."

He was good, Lena had to admit. Very good. The way he painted the scene made her fingers itch to capture it—not just in words, but in images that conveyed the sensual atmosphere he described.

"The bartenders are artists," Adrian continued, his voice dropping to a velvet murmur. "Miko studied under a master mixologist in Tokyo before bringing her talents here. She has this way of reading people—one look and she knows exactly what you need." He leaned slightly closer. "Last month, she created a drink specifically for a woman who'd just defended her doctoral thesis. Called it 'The Dissertation Defense'—smoky mezcal with a bitter chocolate rim and a splash of champagne. The woman cried when she tasted it."

Lena felt a smile tugging at her lips. "That good, huh?"

"That understood," Adrian corrected gently. "That's what The Heel offers that nowhere else does—recognition of who you are, even when you're not sure yourself."

The concealed door, expertly crafted to blend perfectly with the wall, swung open with a soft, almost imperceptible creak, unveiling the staff room hidden behind it. From its dimly lit recesses, Echo emerged, her figure slowly becoming more distinct as she moved into the brighter light of the main area.

"Adrian," she called out, her voice resonating with a clear and commanding presence. "Did that shipment from Veuve arrive?"

"It got here just after lunch, Echo. It's chilling in the wine room," Adrian replied promptly.

Echo—this was the elusive owner, shrouded in an enigmatic aura that seemed to absorb the light around her. Her presence was as ephemeral as a whisper carried by the gentlest breeze, touching the senses with a delicate brush yet leaving an indelible impression. Her movements were fluid, almost ethereal, and her eyes held a depth that promised untold stories. She left a trail of curiosity wherever she went, like the lingering scent of a rare and exotic perfume that beckoned the imagination to follow.

"You must be the writer," Echo remarked, her eyes resting on Lena with a subtle, thoughtful scrutiny. Her eyes, nearly silver, appeared a striking pale gray under the lobby's cozy lights. "Adrian mentioned you'd be chronicling our small haven."

"Lena Marquez, from *Queer Compass*," Lena replied, extending her hand. "Thank you for allowing me access to photograph the Nest."

Echo's handshake was firm but brief. "The Heel has always supported those who support our community." Her smile was cryptic, revealing nothing. "I'm sure Adrian will ensure you experience everything worth writing about."

She gave Adrian a look Lena couldn't quite decipher—it held a hint of amusement, perhaps even mischief, but also something deeper, like shared knowledge of some unspoken secret. Then Echo turned, the burgundy satin of her gown flowing like liquid around her tall frame as she glided toward the elevator.

"Enjoy your stay with us, Ms. Marquez," she called over her shoulder, not bothering to look back. "The storm outside makes our little sanctuary all the more... intimate."

The elevator doors parted for her as if by command rather than technology. She stepped inside, her silhouette a striking contrast against the gold interior. Just before the doors closed, Echo's silver eyes met Lena's once more, a subtle challenge lurking in their depths.

"Do write something... truthful," she said, the words hanging in the air as the doors whispered shut.

Adrian cleared his throat softly. "That's Echo for you. Always making an entrance—and an exit."

"She's..." Lena searched for the right word.

"Exactly," Adrian agreed with a knowing smile. "Most people never find the right word for Echo. That's part of her charm."

Lena watched the floor indicator above the elevator: L... 2... 3... 4. The light stopped at the top floor—Echo's suite, presumably. The pendant at her throat tingled slightly against her skin, and she resisted the urge to touch it, as if Echo might somehow sense the gesture.

"So," Adrian said, interrupting her thoughts. "The Glass Heel tonight? I finish my shift at nine. I could show you around, introduce you to some of the regulars." His tone remained professional, but there was a warmth in his eyes that hadn't been there during their initial meeting—a personal invitation layered beneath the concierge's courtesy.

Lena hesitated, her thumb absently stroking the textured grip of her camera as her mind calculated angles and perspectives like a chess player plotting three moves ahead. The seasoned photojournalist in her—the one who'd once crouched for six hours in the rain to capture the perfect protest shot—recognized that seeing the club with a knowledgeable guide would yield richer, more nuanced material. Adrian clearly navigated The Heel's labyrinthine social ecosystem with the precision of a master cartographer, knowing every shadowed corner and secret doorway. His connections could illuminate stories that would otherwise remain shrouded in the club's velvety darkness.

But beneath her professional calculations lurked something more visceral—a warm flutter that spread from her stomach to her fingertips when Adrian's eyes crinkled at the corners, creating a constellation of fine lines that softened his otherwise perfect composure. The way he'd appeared at her elbow with that steaming burgundy mug precisely when her energy had flagged, the coffee doctored exactly to her preference though she'd never specified it. The slight brush of his fingers against hers when he'd handed her the drink, brief but electric, leaving a ghost of sensation that lingered like the coffee's rich aftertaste.

"I should be taking photos of the club for the article," she reasoned aloud, fingers absently tracing the edge of her camera. "It would be helpful to have someone who knows the place show me around."

"Purely professional," Adrian agreed, though the slight curve of his lips suggested he understood the subtext of her internal debate.

"I'd like that," she decided, glancing at her watch. "Nine works perfectly—gives me time to organize these shots and change."

"Perfect," Adrian said, his smile radiating warmth like the morning sun breaking through clouds. "I'll come to your room at nine, and we can head to the club together."

Chapter 3

Snowbound in the Nest

The blizzard swallowed Chicago whole.

Lena pressed her palm against the frigid glass of her window, feeling the cold seep through her skin as she watched snowflakes transform into horizontal streaks under the assault of howling winds. The city lights, usually a vibrant tapestry of color and life, appeared as hazy, diffused glows through the thickening white curtain. Her phone buzzed again with another emergency alert: all public transportation suspended until further notice.

"So much for 'worst by midnight,'" she muttered, checking the time on her phone. 8:47 PM.

The storm had accelerated with unexpected ferocity, catching even the meteorologists off guard. What had been forecast as a gradual buildup to midnight had instead become a full-blown blizzard before nine. Streets that had been merely snow-dusted when she'd arrived were now invisible under growing drifts that the wind sculpted into otherworldly shapes.

Lena scrolled through the alerts, each one more dire than the last. O'Hare had suspended all flights. Major highways closed indefinitely. The governor had declared a state of emergency for northern Illinois. The words "shelter in place" appeared in bold red letters across her screen.

She swiped away from the alerts and opened her iPhone, quickly typing a text to her editor:

Snowed in at The Heel's Nest. City completely shut down. Silver lining: perfect opportunity for in-depth coverage. Will send preliminary photos tonight.

She attached three of her corridor shots, focusing on the memorial wall portraits, then hit send. The little progress wheel spun for several seconds before confirming delivery. At least the internet was still working.

The thought of being trapped had never particularly bothered Lena. Her job had landed her in far worse situations than being snowed in at a luxury hotel. There was that time in Peru when mudslides had cut off the mountain village she'd been profiling, or the unexpected quarantine in that tiny Greek island pension with the leaky ceiling and spotty electricity.

This, by comparison, was practically a vacation.

Lena turned away from the window and surveyed her half-unpacked suitcase. The black jumpsuit she'd planned to wear to the club lay across the bed, its fabric catching the warm amber light from the bedside lamp. Would Adrian still come at nine, given the worsening conditions? The staff might be needed elsewhere now that the situation had escalated.

A soft knock at the door answered her question.

Lena smoothed her sweater and tucked a strand of hair behind her ear before opening the door. Adrian stood in the hallway, still in his impeccable suit despite the hour and circumstances, though she noticed he'd loosened his tie slightly.

"I thought you might be watching the weather," he said, nodding toward her room where the curtains remained open to the storm. "It's gotten significantly worse in the last hour."

"I noticed," Lena replied, gesturing toward the window. "I was wondering if the club would still be open tonight."

Adrian ran a hand through his hair, a small break in his otherwise composed demeanor. "That's actually why I came by. Most of our staff couldn't make it in, and those who were already here are stuck for the duration." He leaned slightly against the door frame, his shoulders dropping a fraction. "I'll be covering the front desk overnight. Echo's asked everyone to pull double shifts."

"So, no club tour?" Lena tried to keep the disappointment from her voice.

"Not the full experience I promised, I'm afraid." His eyes met hers with genuine regret. "The club is technically open, but it's just Miko behind the bar and our security guard, Darius. No DJ, no dancers. Three very determined regulars made it in before the worst hit, but that's it."

Lena nodded, understanding washing over her. Of course, a skeleton crew would be running things during a weather emergency. It made perfect sense, even if it threw a wrench in her plans.

"How long do you think we'll be snowed in?" she asked.

"The forecast says at least through tomorrow afternoon. The plows can't keep up, and the wind is creating six-foot drifts in some areas." Adrian's gaze drifted to the window behind her, where the snow continued its relentless assault. "We're well-stocked, though. The kitchen has enough supplies for a week, and we keep emergency generators in case the power goes out."

Lena felt a flutter of unexpected excitement. Being trapped here with a handful of people during a blizzard might actually yield better material than a typical club night. There was something intimate about shared isolation, the way it stripped away pretenses and created a temporary community among strangers.

"Mind if I ask you a few questions while you work?" she ventured. "Since I can't experience the full Glass Heel tonight, maybe I could focus on the people who make this place special instead."

Adrian's expression warmed, the professional mask slipping to reveal something more genuine. "I'd enjoy the company, actually. The lobby gets eerily quiet during storms like this." He checked his watch. "I need to be at the desk in a few minutes. Meet me downstairs when you're ready?"

"I'll be down in fifteen," Lena promised.

After Adrian left, she quickly changed her plans. Instead of the glamorous jumpsuit, she opted for comfort—dark jeans and a soft, oversized sweater in deep burgundy that matched the hotel's color scheme. She packed her digital recorder, notebook, and camera into her satchel, then took one last look at the storm raging outside. The city had disappeared entirely now, swallowed by a swirling white void that pressed against her window like a living thing.

When she reached the lobby, Adrian was behind the reception desk, his jacket hung neatly on a coat rack and his sleeves rolled up to his elbows, revealing strong forearms and a simple silver watch. The lobby was dimly lit, with only half the usual lights illuminating the space, creating pools of amber warmth amid lengthening shadows.

"Welcome to the graveyard shift," he said, looking up from the computer screen as Lena approached. "Though I suppose we're all on the graveyard shift tonight."

Lena set her satchel on the polished surface of the desk and pulled out her digital recorder. "Mind if I record our conversation? It's easier than taking notes."

"Not at all." Adrian gestured to a plush armchair near the desk. "Make yourself comfortable. Can I get you anything? Tea, perhaps? I've already had too much coffee today."

"Tea would be perfect." Lena settled into the chair, which enveloped her like a warm embrace. She placed the recorder between them and pressed the red button. "So, Adrian Vega, concierge extraordinaire. How did you end up at The Heel's Nest?"

Adrian's lips curled into a grin as he stepped over to the tiny kitchenette behind the desk. "It's quite a tale. In brief, I needed to transition from working at a budget hotel, and my cousin had a connection to someone who knew Echo." As he touched the electric kettle, it sprang to life with a gentle hum. "The extended version includes a rather uncomfortable interview where I inadvertently drenched Echo's vintage Louboutins with an entire pitcher of water."

Lena raised her eyebrows. "And she hired you anyway?"

"She said anyone who could maintain perfect composure while drenching a pair of four-thousand-dollar shoes had the right temperament for hospitality." He chuckled, the sound warm and genuine. "I think she was testing me, honestly. Echo has... unconventional hiring practices."

"What was your background before this?" Lena leaned forward, genuinely curious.

"Hospitality management at the University of Illinois, but I was on track for corporate hotels—Hilton, Marriott, that world." Adrian selected two tea bags from a wooden box, examining the labels with careful attention. "Chamomile or Earl Grey?"

"Earl Grey, please." Lena watched him prepare the tea with practiced movements. "So what made you choose a boutique hotel instead of the corporate path?"

The kettle clicked off, and Adrian poured steaming water into two midnight-blue mugs identical to the ones they'd used earlier. The rich bergamot aroma wafted through the air as he steeped the tea.

"My family has owned a bakery in Pilsen for three generations," he said, his voice taking on a softer quality. "I grew up watching my *abuelo* remember every customer's name, their children's birthdays, which pastries they preferred. He created this... sanctuary where people felt seen." Adrian's gaze grew distant for a moment. "The corporate hotels wanted me to standardize experiences. Echo wanted me to personalize them."

Lena added honey to her tea, watching the amber liquid swirl as she stirred. This was perfect—Adrian in a reflective mood, the storm isolating them in this pocket of warmth, and her recorder capturing every word. What had started as a logistical setback was transforming into an opportunity for the kind of intimate profile her readers craved.

"What makes The Heel's Nest different from other boutique hotels?" she asked, settling back into the armchair. "Besides the obvious LGBTQ focus."

Adrian leaned against the reception desk, cradling his mug between his palms. "We're not just a hotel with rainbow flags at Pride month. Every aspect of this place was designed by and for queer people." His eyes brightened with genuine passion. "Take the room themes—each one reflects a different facet of queer experience or history. The Muse's Retreat, where you're staying, was inspired by Natalie Clifford Barney's literary salon in Paris."

"The American expatriate who hosted gatherings for queer women writers and artists," Lena nodded, impressed. "I recognized some of the artwork."

"Every detail matters here," Adrian continued. "The towels are oversized because trans guests often prefer more coverage. Our bathroom products are free of gendered marketing. Even the lighting in the rooms was designed to be flattering to all skin tones."

Lena took a sip of her tea, savoring the bergamot's citrusy bite. "What's your favorite part of the job?"

"The stories," Adrian answered without hesitation. "Everyone who walks through that door brings their own narrative. Sometimes they share it with me, sometimes I just glimpse chapters of it." His expression softened. "Last month, we had a couple in their seventies—two women who'd been together since the '60s but married only five years ago. They booked our nicest suite to celebrate their fifty-year anniversary of their first date."

The warmth in his voice made Lena's fingers itch for her camera. This was the kind of authentic moment her readers connected with—not just the glossy façade of a trendy hotel, but the human stories that gave it soul.

"Any memorable guest requests?" she asked, knowing from experience that concierges often had the best anecdotes.

Adrian's laugh was rich and genuine. "Too many to count. There was the guest who needed twenty-four white lilies delivered at exactly midnight for a proposal. Or the famous drag queen—I can't name names—who requested we fill her bathtub with champagne."

"Did you do it?" Lena asked, eyebrows raised.

"Of course not. Do you know how sticky that would be? Not to mention the waste." His eyes crinkled with amusement. "We compromised on champagne service while she soaked in a bath infused with edible gold flakes. Much more practical, equally fabulous."

The wind howled outside, rattling the windows with an eerie persistence that made Lena glance toward the entrance. Snow had piled halfway up the glass door, transforming it into a frosted portal to nowhere.

"What about the rooms themselves?" she asked, steering the conversation back to her research. "Any particularly interesting stories behind them?"

Adrian's face changed subtly, a hint of something—maybe recognition—passed over him before his professional smile reappeared. "Every room has its own theme. The Winter Skin room on the third floor features items pale wood furniture, fur throws, and soft lantern lights. Meanwhile, the Hollywood Seduction room on the second floor includes a dressing-room vanity, stage lights, and a mirrored wall for performances."

"And what about the Rose Room?" Lena kept her tone casual, though this was the room she'd heard whispered about most often in her preliminary research. "I noticed it's the only door with fresh flowers outside."

Adrian's fingers tapped a subtle rhythm against his mug. "You've got a good eye." He set his tea down and leaned forward slightly. "The Rose Room has the most... colorful history of all our suites. It was the first room Echo designed when she acquired the building."

"What makes it special?" Lena pressed, sensing she was approaching something significant.

"Legend has it that Echo herself lived in that room

during the renovation," Adrian said, lowering his voice though they were alone in the lobby. "Before The Heel was The Heel, when this building was just another abandoned factory. She slept on a mattress on the floor while workers transformed the space around her."

Lena's journalistic instincts tingled. "And the roses?"

"They're for Rosalia." Adrian's eyes drifted toward the staircase. "Echo's first love. The story goes that they met at a underground club in the '80s, back when queer spaces were still raids waiting to happen. Rosalia was a dancer—classically trained but working wherever she could. They fell hard and fast."

"What happened to her?" Lena asked, already suspecting the answer wasn't happy from the way Adrian's expression had softened.

"It's all whispers and maybes." Adrian's voice dropped lower, almost reverent. "A prestigious dance company in Paris that couldn't wait. A fight so bitter it shattered everything between them." His fingers traced the rim of his mug. "But the room—that's real. Echo preserves it like a time capsule from '84. Velvet fainting couch. Record player that only spins vinyl. And those roses... she replaces them herself before they can even think about wilting. No one stays there without Echo personally reviewing their reservation."

Lena felt a chill that had nothing to do with the storm outside. "Is it booked tonight?"

"No," Adrian said. "It was occupied last week. Echo herself changes the roses every few days, regardless of whether anyone's staying there."

"Have you always been interested in the hospitality industry?" Lena asked, steering the conversation away from the Rose Room's mysteries. Her journalistic instinct told her there was more to uncover there, but pushing too hard too soon might close doors rather than open them.

Adrian's shoulders relaxed slightly as he settled back against the desk. "I practically grew up in it, though not the luxury end. My family's bakery was my first classroom. I started at eight, folding pastry boxes and sweeping floors. By sixteen, I was handling the morning rush while my *abuelo* worked the ovens."

"From pastries to luxury suites," Lena mused, sipping her tea. "That's quite a journey."

"The fundamentals are the same," Adrian said, his eyes warming with the memory. "It's about anticipating needs before they're spoken. My *abuelo* could tell which customers needed an extra pastry slipped into their bag on hard days, or who needed to be gently steered toward the sugar-free options despite their sweet tooth." He smiled. "I just traded sugar cookies for turndown service."

"What's your favorite part of the job?" she asked, genuinely curious. "Besides the stories."

Adrian considered this, his fingers absently straightening a stack of business cards on the desk. "The moments of transformation. Watching someone walk in carrying the weight of the outside world and then seeing that burden lift as they realize they're truly safe here." His eyes met hers. "It sounds dramatic, but I've seen it happen countless times."

"Any specific examples?" Lena prompted, recognizing the beginning of a story worth capturing.

Adrian hesitated, his gaze drifting to the window where snow continued to pound against the glass. "Actually, I'd rather show you something." He set his mug down with a gentle clink against the polished desk. "Since the storm has effectively closed the club to the public, why not take advantage of the situation?"

"What do you mean?" Lena asked, setting her own tea aside.

"How often do you get to see an empty nightclub?" He smiled, a hint of mischief creeping into his professional demeanor. "I can give you a private tour of The Glass Heel. Just us, no crowds, no performance pressure. The real bones of the place."

Lena felt a flutter of excitement. An exclusive look at the club without the typical nightlife chaos would provide perfect material for her article. "Won't Echo mind?"

"Echo trusts my judgment with guests," Adrian said, straightening his tie. "Besides, you're here to write about the place. Hard to do that without seeing all of it, storm or no storm."

Adrian straightened his tie with a flourish, gesturing toward the unmarked door behind the reception desk. "Care for the backstage tour?" His eyes held a conspiratorial gleam.

Lena nodded, securing her camera across her torso and collecting her bag before following him behind the gleaming reception counter. He guided her toward the discreet doorway she'd spotted employees slipping through earlier.

"This is the staff entrance," Adrian said, pulling a small brass key from his pocket. "It's more discreet than using the main entrance."

The lock yielded with a heavy click, and Adrian eased the door open. They stepped into darkness punctuated only by the red glow of exit signs and faint gleams where light caught metal and glass. Adrian's hand found a switch panel on the wall. Soft illumination revealed a compact staff room with lockers along one wall and a coffee station in the corner. Adrian guided her through a door on the opposite side, past the kitchen's stainless steel expanse, and into the main club. The space wasn't entirely empty—three patrons hunched at the bar where Miko, a bartender with sleeve tattoos visible beneath rolled cuffs, mixed drinks with practiced efficiency.

"Welcome to The Glass Heel," he said softly, stepping aside to let Lena enter first.

Lena stepped into The Glass Heel's emptiness, struck by its quiet dignity. The nightclub revealed itself differently without writhing bodies and thundering bass—architectural secrets normally hidden in darkness and movement. Above, factory beams crossed the high ceiling like black scaffolding, from which crystal pendant lights dangled at staggered heights. They surrounded a disco ball hanging motionless in the center, waiting for life to return.

"Most people never see it like this," Adrian said, his voice carrying in the hushed space despite his low tone. "Empty, I mean. The club has a different personality when it's quiet."

Lena nodded, taking in the expansive dance floor. Its polished wood gleamed under the minimal lighting, reflecting the soft amber glow from the bar like a still lake at sunset. Without dancers' feet scuffing its surface, she could see the intricate inlay work—geometric patterns that radiated outward from the center in a spiral of darker woods, creating a subtle but mesmerizing visual effect.

"Is that original to the building?" she asked, pointing to the floor.

"Echo commissioned it from a local woodworker," Adrian replied. "The pattern is based on the golden ratio. She wanted dancers to feel like they were moving in harmony with something ancient and mathematical."

Lena lifted her camera, framing a shot that captured the spiral pattern disappearing into shadow at the edges. The click of the shutter echoed in the vast space.

"Mind if I take a few more?" she asked, already adjusting her aperture.

"Be my guest," Adrian said, leaning against a nearby column. "The lighting's actually perfect right now. During operating hours, it's usually much darker, with spotlights and strobes."

Lena moved slowly across the floor, capturing the empty stage where performers would normally command attention, the VIP booths with their sumptuous velvet seating arranged in intimate semi-circles, and the ornate brass poles that rose from small satellite stages scattered throughout the space. Each element told part of the story—not just of a nightclub, but of a carefully crafted experience.

"That bar is something else," she said, drawn toward the sweeping counter that anchored the room. Its concrete surface sparkled with embedded mirror fragments, each one catching light like tiny stars across the dark expanse. Behind it, liquor bottles climbed skyward on mirrored shelves, their colored glass creating a kaleidoscope effect. A brass library ladder, complete with ornate wheels and railings, stood ready to access the highest spirits—an elegant anachronism in this modern space.

Adrian followed her gaze. "Echo believes a bar should be both beautiful and functional. The ladder was salvaged from the Chicago Public Library during a renovation in the '90s."

The three patrons huddled at the far end of the bar looked up briefly as Lena approached, then returned to their quiet conversation. Miko, the bartender, nodded in acknowledgment but continued methodically polishing glasses, her tattooed arms moving in hypnotic rhythm.

Lena captured the scene—the solitary bartender, the huddled patrons, the vast emptiness surrounding them—feeling a strange intimacy in this deserted version of what would normally be a vibrant social space.

"Want to see something cool?" Adrian asked, moving

toward a sleek control panel mounted discreetly in the wall near the DJ booth. His fingers hovered over the buttons with familiar confidence.

"Always," Lena replied, lowering her camera.

Adrian pressed a sequence of buttons, and suddenly the room transformed. Soft blue lights faded in along the perimeter of the dance floor, creating an ethereal glow that rippled across the polished wood. The crystal pendant lights dimmed to a warm amber, and the disco ball above began to rotate slowly, sending fractured diamonds of light dancing across the walls and ceiling.

"The lighting system was designed by a Broadway technician," Adrian explained, his face illuminated by the blue glow. "Echo wanted something that could transform the space completely, depending on the mood or event."

Lena turned in a slow circle, watching the play of light across the empty room. It was magical—like being underwater in some bioluminescent grotto. Her camera couldn't possibly capture the full effect, but she lifted it anyway, trying different angles to preserve some essence of the moment.

"It's beautiful," she murmured, lowering her camera again. Some experiences were better lived than documented.

Adrian's fingers moved across the control panel again. "Let me show you one more thing." He pressed another button, and the sound system hummed to life. "Just testing the speakers," he said with a hint of mischief in his voice. "We should make sure everything's functioning properly, right?"

The opening notes of a song Lena recognized filtered through the state-of-the-art sound system—Nina Simone's "Feeling Good." The rich, velvety voice filled the empty club, resonating with perfect acoustics that made it feel as though Nina herself were performing on the silent stage.

"The sound quality is incredible," Lena said, feeling the bass notes vibrate gently through the floorboards.

Adrian stepped away from the control panel and extended his hand toward her. "May I have this dance? It seems a shame to waste such a perfect dance floor when we have it all to ourselves."

Lena hesitated for just a moment, her professional boundaries wavering. But the storm had already blurred those lines, trapping them together in this snow-globe world separate from reality. What was the harm in one dance?

"I should warn you," she said, placing her hand in his, "I'm much better at documenting nightlife than participating in it."

"I find that hard to believe," Adrian replied, gently guiding her to the center of the spiral pattern on the floor. His hand settled at the small of her back, warm and steady. "Just follow my lead."

Nina's voice swelled around them as Adrian began to move, guiding Lena in a simple dance. It wasn't quite a waltz—more fluid, less structured—but his movements were confident and easy to follow. The warmth of his hand against her back radiated through her sweater, and she found herself relaxing into his lead.

"For someone who claims not to participate in nightlife, you move beautifully," Adrian murmured, his voice barely audible above Nina's sultry contralto.

Lena laughed softly. "Years of *quinceañeras* and family weddings. My *tío* Javier insisted all his nieces learn to dance properly."

The disco ball cast spinning fractals of light across Adrian's face, highlighting the strong line of his jaw, the slight curve of his lips as he smiled down at her. Lena became acutely aware of how close they were standing—close enough that she could detect the subtle notes of his cologne mingling with the scent of clean cotton and coffee that clung to his skin.

"Your uncle taught you well," Adrian said, guiding her into a gentle turn that sent her sweater fluttering around her hips.

As Nina's voice soared through the bridge of the song, Adrian's hand pressed slightly more firmly against Lena's back, drawing her incrementally closer. The space between them seemed charged with electricity, a tangible current that made the fine hairs on her arms stand on end despite the warmth of the room.

His eyes held hers, and for a moment, Lena forgot about her article, about the storm, about everything beyond this empty dance floor and the man whose touch seemed to leave trails of heat through the fabric of her sweater. The professional distance she normally maintained with interview subjects evaporated like morning dew under a summer sun.

The song built to its crescendo, and Adrian guided her through one final turn that brought them chest to chest, his breath warm against her temple. For a heartbeat—perhaps two—they remained perfectly still, suspended in the moment as the last notes of the song faded into silence.

Adrian's fingers brushed against hers as the lighting returned to normal, a fleeting contact that sent a small current up Lena's arm. The dance floor, now just polished wood without the magical glow, stretched between them like a neutral territory neither seemed eager to cross.

"I should—" they both began at once, then laughed, the sound easing some of the tension.

"Sorry," Adrian said, running a hand through his hair. "I got carried away with the tour."

"Don't apologize," Lena replied, surprised by the huskiness in her voice. She cleared her throat. "It was... informative."

Something flickered in Adrian's eyes—amusement, perhaps, or recognition of the inadequacy of her word choice. The dance had been many things, but "informative" barely scratched the surface.

"Happy to help," he replied, his formal voice softened by a hint of a smile. "I need to return to the front desk now."

"And I should return to my room to review the photos I captured today."

Adrian reached toward the control panel, his fingers finding the switches with practiced ease. The blue lights faded first, then the golden glow from the bar dimmed until only the exit signs remained, casting their crimson glow across the empty dance floor. The disco ball slowed its rotation, the fractured light patterns disappearing one by one until the room settled into stillness.

"That's enough magic for one night," he said softly, the silence between them suddenly more intimate than their dance had been.

From behind the bar, Miko's voice cut through the darkness. "Giving the private tour, Adrian?" There was something knowing in her tone that made heat rise to Lena's cheeks. "You two want a drink before you head back upstairs?"

"Maybe another time," Adrian replied, his eyes still on Lena.

The three patrons at the far end of the bar continued their hushed conversation, seemingly oblivious to the moment that had just passed on the dance floor. As Lena's eyes adjusted to the dimness, she recognized one of the women—the tall figure with elegant posture and those distinctive black curls cascading down her back. Elena Rodriguez. She'd seen her portrait on the second floor, one of the contemporary photos Adrian had mentioned.

Elena glanced up, catching Lena's gaze across the room. Something passed between them—recognition, perhaps, or simple curiosity—before Elena inclined her head in the slightest of nods and returned to her companions.

"Come on," Adrian said, his hand finding the small of Lena's back again, the touch lighter now but no less electric. "I should show you the way back to your room. The stairs can be tricky in the dark."

He guided her to another section of the club, strategically moving away from the main entrance and the discreet staff door they had slipped through earlier. As they walked, Lena felt a subtle incline beneath her feet, leading them to a staircase that had initially escaped her notice. This staircase was elegantly woven into the club's sophisticated design, its polished steps inviting them upward. The stairs climbed gracefully to a luxurious VIP area, offering an elevated view of the pulsating dance floor below, where lights flickered and shadows danced in rhythm with the music.

Adrian's voice dropped to a whisper that brushed against her ear. "This staircase connects directly to the second floor of the Nest," he said, gesturing toward the elegant steps tucked discreetly into the corner of the VIP section. "Our little secret passage for those with... special access."

Lena's fingers itched for her camera again, but the lighting was too low for a proper shot. Besides, something about this moment felt too intimate for documentation—the hidden stairway, Adrian's hand at her elbow, the lingering echo of their dance.

"The hotel and club are more connected than I

realized," she said, following him onto the first step. The stair illuminated beneath her foot, a soft amber glow that appeared only as she moved onto it, then faded once she advanced to the next.

"That's by design," Adrian replied, his shoulder brushing against hers as they ascended. "Echo believed in seamless transitions between worlds." The stairs delivered them to the second-floor hallway where the gallery of photographs began—faces of the Heel's most devoted clientele captured in silver halide, with Carmen Rodriguez's portrait commanding attention nearest the stairwell.

"If you need anything else tonight, you know where to find me," Adrian said, his professional tone not quite masking the warmth underneath.

They parted at the stairwell, Adrian heading toward the elevator while Lena lingered, her gaze following his retreating form. A flutter of uncertainty settled in her stomach as she turned toward the stairs, each step up to the third floor giving her time to question exactly what line she had just crossed.

Chapter 4

Concierge Room Service

The lights died with a soft gasp.

Lena froze, her fingers hovering over her laptop's keyboard as darkness swallowed her room. For three heartbeats, The Muse's Retreat existed in perfect blackness—no glow from the bedside lamp, no hum from the heating system, no blue light from her laptop screen. Just the sound of her own breathing and the distant howl of the blizzard battering the windows.

Then, with a quiet whir, emergency lights flickered on. A soft amber glow emanated from recessed fixtures near the baseboards, casting long shadows across the walls. Her laptop screen blinked back to life, the battery having taken over seamlessly.

"Well, that's ominous," she muttered, saving the document where she'd been organizing her notes on The Heel's Nest. The power outage couldn't have lasted more than a few seconds, but it left her feeling oddly unsettled.

Something about the abrupt silence, the way the darkness had seemed almost alive—hungry—before the emergency lights pushed it back.

She glanced at her phone. 11:43 PM. After their dance in the empty club and the strange electricity that had hummed between them, she'd retreated to her room, determined to maintain some professional distance. Adrian had returned to his post at the reception desk, and she'd thrown herself into work, sorting through photographs and jotting down impressions while they were still fresh.

The main lights flickered twice more before stabilizing, the chandelier above her bed resuming its warm glow as if nothing had happened. Lena closed her laptop and stretched, rolling her shoulders to release the tension that had built there. The storm outside showed no signs of abating—if anything, it seemed to be intensifying, the wind shrieking against the glass like something wounded and furious.

A soft ping from her phone drew her attention. A text from her editor: *Love the corridor shots. The memorial wall is perfect for our Pride issue sidebar. Get me more of the personal stories behind the place.*

Personal stories. Like Adrian's journey from his family's bakery to this luxurious sanctuary. Like Echo's mysterious past with Rosalia and the room that remained a shrine to lost love.

Lena chewed her lower lip, considering. She'd planned to stay in for the night, but the power flicker had left her restless. Maybe a walk would clear her head. And if that walk happened to take her past the reception desk where Adrian was working the overnight shift...well, that was just good journalism.

Lena fished Adrian's business card from her wallet and punched the number into her phone. He answered on the second ring.

"Midnight inspiration keeping you up?" His voice carried a smile.

"The article draft," she said, tracing circles on her bedspread. "And I wanted to check about those lights."

"Just a hiccup. Emergency generators kicked in perfectly. Main power should be back soon." He paused. "Can I bring you something from downstairs? Kitchen's still functional."

"That would be lovely. Maybe a sandwich and chamomile, if you have it?"

"On my way," he said, and the line went quiet.

A few minutes later, the elevator dinged, and Echo emerged into the lobby, her dark hair sprinkled with melting snowflakes.

"We've got enough fuel for the generators to last three or four days," she stated.

Adrian's eyes grew wide. "Please tell me you didn't climb up to the roof in this blizzard."

Echo gave a slight smile. "It had to be done by someone."

She brushed the snow off her shoulders, the ice crystals vanishing quickly from the warmth of her skin. Her black dress hugged her figure, untouched by her winter journey. Her silver-gray eyes observed Adrian.

"I notice you've found a guest worthy of headlines to keep you company during the storm," Echo remarked, her melodious voice echoing across the lobby. A knowing smile danced at the corners of her red lips as she glanced between them. "Be cautious, Adrian. Journalists have a knack for digging up all sorts of... surprising stories."

Adrian's cheeks reddened slightly. "Ms. Marquez is gathering information for her article. I was just providing some room service since the kitchen is still running."

"Of course you were. Miko mentioned your dance with Ms. Marquez to me," Echo's laugh was like warm honey on ice. "Always the ultimate professional."

The power flickered, the lights dimming briefly before steadying.

"I should probably check on the generators again," Echo said, though she didn't head to the door. Instead, she ran her fingers along the reception desk's edge. "The blizzard looks quite spectacular from the rooftop. The entire city appears wild and ancient."

Echo glided toward the elevator, her footsteps silent against the marble floor. After she disappeared behind the closing doors, Adrian slipped through the concealed staff entrance to prepare Lena's late-night provisions.

Lena stared at the ceiling of The Muse's Retreat, watching shadows dance across the ornate plasterwork. Her stomach growled, reminding her that she'd skipped dinner in favor of working. The storm's constant howl formed a strange lullaby, almost hypnotic in its intensity.

A firm knock at her door startled her from her thoughts.

She padded across the room in her sock feet, the plush carpet cushioning each step. When she opened the door, Adrian stood there balancing a covered tray, his tie loosened and the top button of his shirt undone.

"Room service," he said with a smile that crinkled the corners of his eyes. "One midnight snack as requested."

"You're a lifesaver," Lena said, stepping back to let him enter. "I didn't realize how hungry I was until I smelled whatever you've brought."

Adrian set the tray on the small table near the window. When he lifted the silver dome, the aroma of toasted bread and melted cheese filled the room. "Club kitchen special—grilled brie with fig jam on sourdough, and a side of rosemary sweet potato fries. And your chamomile tea."

Lena's mouth watered at the sight. "That looks way better than the sandwich I was expecting."

"Miko insisted. She said, and I quote, 'Nobody gets a basic sandwich during a blizzard apocalypse.'" Adrian arranged the plate and teacup with practiced precision. "She has strong opinions about comfort food."

"Please thank her for me," Lena said, moving toward the table. "Would you... like to join me? There's enough here for two."

Adrian hesitated, his fingers lingering on the edge of the tray. "I shouldn't leave the desk unattended for too long."

"Who's going to check in during a blizzard?" Lena asked, raising an eyebrow. "Besides, this is part of my research. I need to know what kind of food The Heel's Nest serves its guests."

A smile tugged at the corner of his mouth. "When you put it that way, it would be unprofessional of me to refuse."

He pulled out a chair for her before taking the seat opposite, their knees almost touching beneath the small table. Lena broke the sandwich in half, the melted cheese stretching between the pieces in gooey strands.

"So," she said, passing him his portion, "tell me about the power outage. Does that happen often during storms?"

Their fingers brushed as he accepted the sandwich, sending a small jolt up her arm that had nothing to do with static electricity.

"The old building has its peculiarities," Adrian said softly, his voice resonating warmly in the cozy room. "I think the storm might have caused a power outage, though this isn't typical during a storm. This blizzard is the worst I've encountered in several years."

Lena took a bite of her sandwich, the perfect blend of crispy bread and creamy brie melting on her tongue. The fig jam added a sweet counterpoint that made her close her eyes for a moment in appreciation.

"We should move to the couch," she suggested, gathering her plate and tea. "More comfortable than these chairs."

Adrian followed with his portion of the sandwich, settling beside her on the plush velvet sofa. The cushions dipped beneath their weight, bringing them closer together than either had perhaps intended. Their knees touched, a warm point of contact that Lena found herself acutely aware of.

"So you mentioned this building has peculiarities," she prompted, taking another bite of her sandwich to hide the slight catch in her breath when Adrian shifted, his leg pressing more firmly against hers.

"It's over a hundred years old," he said, his voice lower now that they sat so close. "Echo preserved as much of the original architecture as possible during the renovation. The electrical system is modern, but it interacts with the old bones of the place in... interesting ways."

Lena sipped her chamomile tea, the steam warming her face. "What was it before The Heel?"

"A textile factory, then a warehouse, then nothing for almost two decades." Adrian's eyes caught the amber light from the lamp, turning them to liquid gold. "Echo saw potential where everyone else saw decay."

"She seems to have a gift for that," Lena observed, noticing how Adrian's shoulders had relaxed, his body angling subtly toward hers. "Seeing value in the overlooked."

"It extends to people too," he said, his gaze dropping briefly to where their knees touched before meeting her eyes again. "Half the staff here were considered unhirable elsewhere for one reason or another. Echo has a sixth sense for hidden talents."

"Including yours?" Lena asked, setting her empty plate on the coffee table.

Adrian smiled, a genuine expression that transformed his face from merely handsome to something that made her heart stutter. "I spilled water on her shoes, remember? Not exactly showcasing my talents."

"And yet she hired you anyway." Lena tucked one leg beneath her, turning to face him more fully. Their knees remained pressed together, neither making any move to create distance. "What did she see that day?"

Adrian considered this, absently running his thumb along the edge of his plate. "She asked me a question after I soaked her shoes. She said, 'What would you do if a guest had a crisis at 3 AM that wasn't covered in any training manual?'"

"What did you say?" Lena found herself leaning closer, drawn in by the quiet intimacy of his voice.

"I told her I'd handle it the way my *abuelo* would—with dignity, discretion, and the understanding that people are never more vulnerable than when they're away from home." His voice had softened, and Lena could almost see the young man he must have been, earnest and determined in that interview. She found herself smiling back at him, the professional wall she usually maintained with sources crumbling a little more with each passing second.

"Echo hired me on the spot," Adrian continued, his voice a low rumble that seemed to vibrate through the point where their knees touched. "Said she'd never heard a more honest answer in her life."

Lena nodded, suddenly aware of how close they'd drifted toward each other. The couch cushions had betrayed them, creating a subtle valley that drew them together like planets caught in each other's gravity. Her laptop and recorder lay forgotten on the coffee table—this had stopped being an interview minutes ago, though she wasn't sure exactly when the shift had occurred.

"More sweet potato fry?" Adrian offered, holding out the plate between them.

"Thanks," she said, her fingers brushing against his as she selected a crispy fry dusted with rosemary salt. The contact sent a small current up her arm, and she wondered if he felt it too.

The wind howled outside, rattling the windows with renewed fury. The storm had created a cocoon around them, isolating this room—this moment—from the rest of the world. The usual rules seemed suspended, existing in some distant reality beyond the swirling snow.

"What about you?" Adrian asked, his voice gentle. "What made you choose travel journalism?"

Lena dipped her fry in the remaining fig jam, considering the question. "I've always been restless," she admitted. "Even as a kid, I was always packing imaginary suitcases, planning escapes."

"What were you escaping from?" His question held no judgment, only curiosity.

"Expectations, mostly." Lena tucked a strand of hair behind her ear. "My family had very specific ideas about success—doctor, lawyer, engineer. Not exactly 'professional wanderer with a camera.'"

Adrian's laugh was warm, and she found herself studying the curve of his smile, the way it transformed his entire face. A small dimple appeared in his right cheek, visible only when his smile reached its fullest expression.

"And how did they take it when you chose journalism?" he asked, reaching for his tea. Their fingers brushed again as she passed him the cup, and this time she was certain the contact lingered a fraction longer than necessary.

"My mother still introduces me as 'my daughter who takes pictures for magazines, but she's very smart—she could have been a doctor.'" Lena rolled her eyes, but there was fondness in her voice. "They've come around, though. My *abuela* has a scrapbook of all my published pieces."

"That's sweet," Adrian said, his smile softening. "Family support matters, even when it comes with strings attached."

Lena nodded, amazed at how naturally the conversation unfolded between them. This wasn't the usual scripted interaction of journalist and source she was used to. "Honestly, they were more upset when I said I wanted to pursue travel journalism than when I came out as transgender."

Adrian's expression remained soft, attentive. "Thank you for sharing that with me." He reached for the plate, sliding it closer to her.

"It's easy to talk to you," Lena admitted. Their hands brushed as they both reached for the last sweet potato fry, and she felt that same electric current race up her arm. She pulled back, gesturing for him to take it. "You have it."

"We could share," he suggested, breaking the fry in half. His fingers grazed hers as he placed the piece in her palm, the contact brief but deliberate.

The warmth of his skin lingered against hers. Lena found herself studying his face as he ate his portion—the strong line of his jaw, the slight shadow of stubble appearing as the night wore on, and that smile that transformed his features from merely handsome to something that made her pulse quicken. The small dimple in his right cheek appeared again, and she had to resist the urge to reach out and touch it.

"You have a crumb," Adrian said softly, his voice dropping to just above a whisper. He leaned closer, his eyes fixed on a point near the corner of her mouth. "Just there."

Lena's breath caught as he raised his hand, his thumb hovering near her lower lip. Time seemed to slow, the howling storm outside fading to a distant murmur as the space between them charged with unspoken possibility.

His thumb gently brushed against the corner of her mouth, removing the crumb with a touch so light it felt like a whisper against her skin. But instead of pulling away, he lingered, his gaze dropping to her lips.

Lena leaned forward slightly—an almost imperceptible movement, but it was enough. The distance between them vanished as Adrian closed the final gap, his lips meeting hers in a kiss that was tentative at first, a question rather than a statement. His mouth was warm, tasting faintly of fig jam and chamomile, and Lena found herself answering his unspoken question by returning the pressure, her hand coming to rest lightly against his chest.

The kiss deepened, growing more certain but remaining gentle, an exploration rather than a conquest. Lena's eyes fluttered closed as she surrendered to the sensation, the warmth spreading through her body like honey in hot tea. Adrian's hand moved to cup her cheek, his touch reverent, as if she were something precious he'd discovered.

When they finally pulled apart, it was only by inches. Lena could feel the soft exhale of his breath against her lips, could see the question forming in his eyes—was this okay? Had he crossed a line?

"I'm not normally so..." Adrian began, his voice husky.

"Me neither," Lena whispered, her hand still resting against the solid warmth of his chest, feeling his heartbeat beneath her palm. "But there's something about blizzards that makes everything feel like an alternate reality," she finished, unable to look away from his eyes.

The moment hung between them, delicate as blown glass. Adrian's thumb traced a gentle arc along her cheekbone, his touch feather-light. Time seemed suspended, the howling storm creating a pocket universe where only they existed.

Then Adrian pulled back, the warmth of his hand leaving her face. He cleared his throat and stood, straightening his tie with fingers that weren't quite steady.

"I should get back to the desk," he said, his voice rougher than before. "Concierge code, you know. Rule number one: don't kiss the guests, no matter how compelling they might be."

Lena felt heat rise to her cheeks. "Is that really rule number one?"

"It's definitely in the top five," Adrian replied, a smile tugging at the corner of his mouth despite his obvious attempt to regain his professional composure. "Right after 'never reveal the secret coffee blend.'"

Lena laughed, the sound breaking some of the tension that hummed between them. "Serious breach of protocol, then."

"Worth it," Adrian said softly, his eyes meeting hers with an intensity that made her breath catch again. He gathered the empty plates and cups, arranging them neatly on the tray. "But I really should go. The night shift doesn't watch itself."

Lena nodded, rising to walk him to the door. "Thank you for the midnight snack. And the company."

Adrian paused at the threshold, tray balanced in one

hand. "Sleep well, Lena." The way he said her name—soft, almost reverent—sent a shiver down her spine that had nothing to do with the storm raging outside.

After he left, Lena pressed her fingertips to her lips, still feeling the ghost of his kiss. She moved to the window, watching the snow swirl in hypnotic patterns against the glass. The city beyond was invisible now, swallowed by white. The storm had cut them off from the world, creating this strange liminal space where normal rules seemed suspended.

Chapter 5

Silence of Snow

Lena woke to the gentle tap of knuckles against wood.

Consciousness returned in stages—first the warmth of blankets, then the distant howl of wind, and finally the realization that someone was at her door. Morning light diffused through the curtains, painting the room in soft blues and grays. She blinked, disoriented, the memory of last night's kiss floating to the surface of her mind like a dream.

"Just a minute," she called, her voice thick with sleep. She fumbled for her phone on the nightstand. 7:43 AM. Earlier than she'd planned to wake after their late-night conversation.

She slipped from beneath the covers, shivering as her bare feet met the cool floor. Grabbing the hotel's plush robe from the foot of the bed, she wrapped it around herself and padded to the door, finger-combing her hair into some semblance of order.

When she opened the door, Adrian stood there holding two steaming mugs, looking unfairly put-together for the early hour. His charcoal suit had been replaced by dark jeans and a navy sweater that made his eyes seem deeper, warmer somehow.

"Morning delivery," he said, his voice low and rich. "I thought you might need caffeine after our late night."

Lena felt heat rise to her cheeks at the memory of his lips against hers. "You're a mind reader," she said, stepping back to let him enter. "Though I didn't expect personal delivery service."

"Concierge premium service," Adrian replied with a hint of mischief in his smile. "Only available during record-breaking blizzards." He handed her a mug—the same midnight-blue ceramic from yesterday—and she wrapped her fingers around it, savoring the warmth.

The rich aroma of freshly brewed coffee filled her nostrils, complex notes of chocolate and spice promising the perfect first sip. She inhaled deeply, letting the scent chase away the last cobwebs of sleep.

"The storm's still going?" she asked, moving to the window and pulling back the curtain.

"Technically it stopped around 4 AM," Adrian said, coming to stand beside her. "But we've got about ten inches of accumulation, and nothing's moving out there. The plows can't keep up."

Outside, Chicago had vanished beneath a pristine blanket of white. The usual urban cacophony was silenced, replaced by an eerie stillness that made the city seem abandoned. No cars moved on the streets below, their shapes mere lumps beneath the snow. The sidewalks had disappeared completely, and the only marks disturbing the perfect white expanse were the meandering trails of a few ambitious birds.

"It's beautiful," Lena murmured, taking a sip of her coffee. The liquid was hot and perfect—dark and rich with just a hint of cinnamon that lingered on her tongue. "And slightly apocalyptic."

"Thought we might go see it up close," Adrian said, his eyes reflecting the snow-light from the window. "The ground floor entrance leads right out to the street. It needs to be shoveled and cleaned. There's something almost magical about a city completely silenced by snow."

Lena glanced down at her robe, suddenly aware of her state of undress. "Give me five minutes to change?"

"Take your time. I'll wait in the hallway."

When Adrian stepped out, Lena moved quickly, pulling on jeans and a thick cream sweater. She brushed her teeth, splashed water on her face, and ran a comb through her dark hair, deciding to leave it loose around her shoulders. A touch of tinted lip balm was her only concession to makeup—it seemed pointless to put on a full face just to get it wind-chapped.

Adrian was leaning against the wall when she emerged, still holding his coffee mug. His eyes traveled over her with quiet appreciation.

"That was fast," he said.

"Travel writer skills. I can be packed and ready in under ten minutes in any time zone." She locked her door and pocketed the key. "Lead the way to this winter wonderland."

They rode the elevator to the lobby, where the morning sun streamed through the windows, creating long shadows on the shiny floor. Adrian placed their empty mugs on the reception desk, then exited through the door she had come in through the previous day. He removed his coat from a hook by the door and picked up the snow shovel and a bag of salt.

"Here," Adrian said, offering her a pair of thick gloves from a drawer near the door. "You'll need these."

Lena slipped the gloves on, noticing they were slightly too large but lined with soft fleece that immediately warmed her fingers. Adrian unlocked the front door, and a blast of frigid air rushed in, carrying with it a few dancing snowflakes. He stepped out first, pushing against the door as snow crunched beneath his boots.

"Careful," he warned, extending his hand to help her navigate the small drift that had formed against the threshold.

Lena took his hand, grateful for the support as she stepped into a world transformed. The familiar urban landscape had vanished, replaced by sweeping curves of pristine white. Buildings stood like islands in a frozen sea, their edges softened by snow. The usual city soundtrack—traffic, voices, construction—had been replaced by an almost holy silence, broken only by the crystalline crunch of their footsteps.

"Oh," she breathed, her exhale forming a cloud that hung in the air before dissipating. "It's like a different planet."

Adrian smiled, his breath creating similar clouds. "It only happens once or twice a winter—this perfect moment before the plows and salt trucks ruin everything."

The cold bit at Lena's exposed neck, and she shivered, wishing she'd thought to bring a scarf. As if reading her mind, Adrian unwound the navy cashmere scarf from around his own neck.

"Here," he said, stepping closer. "You're underdressed for arctic exploration."

Before she could protest, he draped the scarf around her neck, his fingers brushing against her skin as he wrapped it securely. The wool carried his warmth and scent—that same subtle cologne she'd noticed during their dance, mixed with coffee and something uniquely him.

"Won't you be cold?" she asked, already knowing the answer as he picked up the shovel.

"I run hot," he replied with a small smile, plunging the shovel into the snow covering the entrance. "Besides, shoveling warms you up fast."

Lena watched as he carved a path through the snow, his movements efficient and practiced. The muscles in his back shifted beneath his coat as he lifted each shovelful and tossed it aside, creating small mountains along the edge of his clearing. The physical labor brought color to his cheeks and a gleam to his eyes that made her stomach flutter.

"So," she said, stepping carefully along the path he'd created, "do you always personally shovel the sidewalk, or is this special blizzard duty?"

Adrian paused, leaning on the shovel handle. "Normally we have a service, but they won't be able to get here until the main roads are cleared. And we can't exactly have guests wading through knee-deep snow."

"Bold of you to assume there are guests who want to leave this cozy sanctuary," Lena said, gesturing back toward the building with a smile playing on her lips.

"Fair point," Adrian conceded, resuming his work. The shovel scraped rhythmically against the concrete as he cleared a wider path. "Though I imagine Miko might want to go home eventually. She's been here since yesterday morning."

Lena pulled Adrian's scarf higher, burying her nose in its soft folds. The cashmere smelled like him—a subtle blend of cedar and something warmer, more personal. She watched as he worked methodically, his breaths forming small clouds in the frigid air.

"How long have you worked at The Heel?" she asked, stepping carefully along the path he'd created.

"Almost five years now," he replied between shovelfuls. "Started as night manager, worked my way up to head concierge in about eighteen months."

"Fast track," Lena observed, admiring the efficient way he carved through the snow. "Echo must have seen something special in you."

Adrian paused, resting his weight against the shovel. "Echo has a gift for seeing people's potential, sometimes before they see it themselves." He looked up at the snow-covered building, his expression thoughtful. "This place was a wreck when she bought it—water damage, structural issues, you name it. Everyone told her it was a money pit, but she saw what it could become."

"Some say it used to be a speakeasy during Prohibition," Adrian continued, resuming his rhythmic shoveling. "There's a hidden room in the basement with old bottles still embedded in the walls. Echo preserved it as a kind of time capsule."

Lena wrapped her arms around herself, fascinated by the way his words created little clouds in the frigid air. "That's incredible. Was it always a queer space?"

"Not officially, but the rumors suggest it was a gathering place for people who didn't fit neatly into society's boxes even back then." Adrian paused to catch his breath, leaning on the shovel. "The previous owner before Echo was an elderly woman who ran it as a boarding house in the seventies and eighties. She apparently had a 'don't ask, don't tell' policy long before the military coined the term."

The snow crunched beneath Lena's boots as she shifted her weight. "So The Heel has always been a sanctuary of sorts."

"In different forms, yes." Adrian's shovel bit into another drift, carving a clean path. "Echo has stories from the old-timers who used to visit—drag queens who would arrive in men's clothing and transform in the bathrooms, couples who could only be themselves behind these walls."

He worked in silence for a moment, his breath forming rhythmic clouds. The only sounds were the scrape of metal against concrete and the distant howl of wind around building corners.

"There are other stories too," he said, his voice dropping lower. "The kind that probably wouldn't be suitable for your article."

Lena's interest piqued immediately. "What kind of stories?"

Adrian's cheeks reddened slightly, though whether from exertion or the topic, she couldn't tell. "Let's just say The Heel's Nest has always catered to people seeking... experiences they couldn't find elsewhere." He cleared his throat. "What happens in those rooms is best left for only the walls to know about."

"You're being cryptic," Lena said, a smile playing at her lips despite the cold biting at her cheeks.

"Deliberately so." Adrian's eyes met hers, amusement mingling with something more serious. "Part of what makes this place special is the privacy we guarantee. Some guests come here precisely because they can explore aspects of themselves they keep hidden elsewhere."

He resumed shoveling, his movements creating a rhythm that seemed to punctuate his words. "The Rose Room alone has seen decades of secret rendezvous—politicians with their real lovers, celebrities escaping the spotlight, people discovering parts of themselves they never knew existed."

"Now you're just teasing me with stories I can't publish," Lena said, watching as he cleared another section of sidewalk.

Adrian laughed, the sound bright in the winter stillness. "Consider it background information. The soul of The Heel isn't in its famous guests or scandalous encounters—it's in being a place where people can be authentic without judgment." Adrian paused, leaning on his shovel as he gazed at the transformed street. "It has always been a sanctuary, especially for those who are transgender and the people who admire them."

The words wrapped around Lena like a cozy blanket, providing warmth despite the biting cold that nipped at her skin. She shifted from foot to foot, her boots crunching against the frost-covered ground, eager to do more than simply stand there and watch him toil.

"Let me do something," she said, gesturing to the bag of salt he'd brought out. "I can at least salt the areas you've already cleared."

Adrian nodded, seeming grateful for the offer. "That would be helpful. Just sprinkle it evenly—not too much or it'll damage the concrete."

Lena grabbed the bag, surprised by its weight, and began scattering salt across the freshly shoveled path. The crystals glittered in the morning light as they hit the wet concrete, already beginning to melt the thin layer of ice beneath.

"Echo's mentor was a transgender woman named Vivian," Adrian went on while navigating another drift. "She operated an underground club in Boystown during the '70s and '80s. When Vivian passed away due to complications from HIV, she left Echo with enough funds to establish her own venue."

Lena worked methodically, following behind Adrian's cleared path with her trail of salt. "So The Heel was born from that legacy?"

"Exactly." Adrian's breath clouded in the frigid air. "Echo wanted to create something that honored Vivian but took the concept further—not just a club, but a complete sanctuary. A place where trans women especially could feel not just tolerated, but celebrated."

The salt bag grew lighter as Lena continued her work, her fingers growing numb despite the gloves. "That explains the portraits in the hallway."

"Our history wall," Adrian nodded, his cheeks reddened from exertion and cold. "Echo believes in honoring those who came before, who made places like this possible. Some of those women paid with their lives just for existing."

They worked in companionable silence for a few minutes, the only sounds the scrape of the shovel and the soft patter of salt hitting concrete. A cardinal landed on a nearby snow-covered bush, its brilliant red plumage a shocking contrast against the white landscape.

"When I first started transitioning," Lena said, her voice soft against the winter stillness, "I couldn't find places where I felt safe. Especially traveling for work." She scattered another handful of salt, watching it dissolve into the wet concrete. "That's why I started writing specifically for *Queer Compass*. I wanted to create a resource I wished I'd had."

Adrian paused, resting on his shovel again. His eyes met hers with quiet understanding. "And now you're helping others find their sanctuaries."

"Trying to," she said with a small smile.

"Well, you've found one here," Adrian replied, resuming his shoveling with renewed vigor. "Echo made sure of that. The Heel is more than just a place to stay or party—it's a living testament to our community's resilience."

The bitter cold had begun to seep through Lena's layers like water through tissue paper, turning her fingers into clumsy, aching appendages despite her wool-lined leather gloves. She flexed them uselessly, wincing as pins and needles shot through her knuckles. Adrian's gaze flickered toward her reddened cheeks and the slight tremble in her shoulders. He straightened up from his hunched position over the shovel, rolling his broad shoulders beneath his heavy coat as he examined their handiwork—a glistening pathway carved through the pristine snow, the salt crystals already melting tiny constellations into the ice.

"We've done enough for now," he said, planting the shovel in a nearby snowbank. "Let's get you back inside before you freeze."

They retraced their steps to the entrance, boots leaving paired impressions in the fresh snow. Adrian held the heavy oak door open for her, its brass hinges groaning against the cold. The lobby's amber warmth enveloped Lena like a lover's embrace, thawing her wind-chapped cheeks and frost-nipped ears. Heat crawled back into her extremities, bringing a rush of prickling pins and needles to her bluish fingertips. She unwound Adrian's scarf from her neck—forest-green cashmere with hand-knotted fringe—the fabric still carrying his scent of cedar and something distinctly masculine she couldn't name but instantly recognized.

"Keep it for now," he said when she tried to hand it back. "You might need it again later."

As they stepped into the Nest's spacious lobby, their footsteps echoing softly against the polished marble floor, they headed toward the gleaming elevator doors. The warm glow of soft lighting cast gentle shadows across the room, highlighting three figures comfortably seated in plush, high-backed chairs. These were the snowed-in guests they had met the previous night, their faces now familiar, framed by the cozy ambiance of the lobby.

Lena recognized Elena Rodriguez instantly—the six-foot-tall professional dancer whose commanding presence dominated even from the plush armchair where she now sat, one long leg crossed elegantly over the other, fingers adorned with vintage silver rings drumming lightly against the armrest as if keeping time to some private melody.

"Adrian!" Elena called, her voice warm and rich. "I see you've been playing in the snow." Her eyes flickered to Lena with undisguised interest, a knowing smile playing at the corners of her mouth. "And you've found company."

"Ms. Rodriguez," Adrian nodded, his professional demeanor sliding back into place though his eyes retained their warmth. "This is Lena Marquez from *Queer Compass*. She's doing a feature on The Heel's Nest."

"A journalist! How exciting," Elena extended her free hand, her grip firm and confident when Lena shook it. "Though I suspect journalism isn't all you've been doing during our little weather emergency." Her eyes danced with mischief as she glanced between them. "Nothing brings people together quite like a blizzard, does it? I've always found storm romances to be the most... intense."

Heat rushed to Lena's cheeks. "We were just clearing the entrance," she said, gesturing vaguely toward the lobby door.

"Of course you were, darling." Elena's laugh was melodious, without a hint of mockery. "David and Michelle here were just 'playing chess' all night in the Blush Desire Room." She winked at the couple beside her, who exchanged amused glances.

"The storm has certainly created some unexpected connections," said David, extending his hand to Lena to shake. She smiled, the warmth of connection thawing the last of the cold from her fingertips.

"These storms are notorious for starting romances," Elena added with a theatrical sigh. "Something about being trapped together with nowhere to run..."

Adrian cleared his throat. "We were about to head back upstairs. Can I get anyone coffee or tea before I go?"

"Actually," Lena said, the idea forming as Elena's words hung in the air, "I'd love to interview all of you if you have a few minutes." She gestured to her leather satchel. "Part of my article is capturing the authentic experiences of guests. What better perspective than people weathering the storm here?"

Elena's face lit up with delight. "A captive audience becomes the captive storytellers! I love it." She patted the empty armchair beside her. "Come, sit. I have stories that would make your readers blush."

"I'd be happy to contribute," Michelle added, leaning forward with interest. Her auburn hair fell in soft waves around her face as she smiled at Lena. "We've been coming to The Heel for years."

Lena glanced at Adrian, who nodded encouragingly. "I'll grab us all some coffee while you set up," he offered, already moving toward the concealed staff door.

"Perfect," Lena said, settling into one of the remaining armchairs and pulling out her digital recorder and notebook. The chair enveloped her in plush comfort, the fabric warm against her back still chilled from their outdoor excursion. She placed the recorder on the coffee table between them. "Do you mind if I record our conversation? It helps me capture quotes accurately."

"Record away, darling," Elena said with a dismissive wave of her bejeweled hand. "I'm used to having my every word preserved for posterity."

Adrian returned with a tray of steaming mugs and a plate of pastries that sent a wave of buttery sweetness through the air. He distributed the coffee before taking the last empty chair next to Lena, their knees almost touching in the intimate circle they'd formed.

"So," Lena began, warming her hands around the midnight-blue ceramic mug, "how did each of you first discover The Heel's Nest?"

Elena leaned forward, her eyes sparkling. "I was here opening night, before most people even knew it existed. Echo and I danced together in Chicago back in the day." She took a delicate sip of her coffee. "When she told me she was opening a sanctuary for our community, I knew it would be something special."

"You're a dancer?" Lena asked.

"Was, am, will always be," Elena corrected with a graceful flick of her wrist. "Though these days I teach more than perform. My studio is just three blocks from here."

Lena jotted a quick note, feeling the weight of Adrian's gaze on her profile. The warmth from their shared outdoor excursion still lingered between them, a secret current beneath the professional veneer of this impromptu interview.

"And you two?" Lena turned to David and Michelle. "What brings you to The Glass Heel?" Lena asked, pulling out her notebook and pen, the recorder already capturing their voices. The warmth of the lobby wrapped around them like a cocoon, a stark contrast to the frozen landscape outside.

Michelle and David exchanged a glance, their silent communication hinting at years of shared understanding. Michelle tucked a strand of auburn hair behind her ear, her brown eyes crinkling at the corners as she smiled.

"We actually stumbled upon it by accident," she said, her voice melodious with a slight rasp that gave it character. "It was about seven years ago, wasn't it, David?"

David nodded, his hazel eyes warm as he looked at his wife. "We were celebrating our twenty-third anniversary, and our original dinner reservation fell through because of a kitchen fire."

"We were wandering the neighborhood, getting increasingly hangry," Michelle continued with a laugh that seemed to brighten the entire lobby. "Then we saw this discrete entrance, and something about it just called to us."

Lena leaned forward, intrigued. The leather of her notebook creaked softly as she flipped to a fresh page. "And what was your first impression when you walked in?"

"That we had finally found a place to call home," Michelle stated plainly, her fingers lacing with David's. "By then, I had been transitioning for nearly thirty years, and although we had discovered some accepting communities, there was always this... unease whenever we stepped into new environments."

"But not here," David added, his voice deep and steady. "Echo greeted us personally that night, took one look at Michelle, and said, 'Finally, someone worthy of our best table.'"

Lena's pen moved quickly across the page, capturing the warmth in their voices, the way they finished each other's thoughts. The recorder hummed quietly on the table between them, a silent witness to their story.

"We've been regulars ever since," Michelle said. "At least twice a month, sometimes more."

"And have you stayed in the Heel's Nest before, or do you usually just visit the club?" Lena asked, glancing briefly at Adrian, who was watching the exchange with quiet interest, his long fingers wrapped around his mug.

"Oh, we've stayed several times," Michelle's eyes sparkled with mischief. "The Blush Desire Room is our favorite, though we've tried most of them over the years."

David cleared his throat, a hint of color rising to his cheeks. "Each room has its own... personality. Echo has a gift for creating spaces that feel both luxurious and deeply intimate."

"And what about the Heel's Nest specifically interests you for your article?" Elena interjected, her elegant fingers tapping lightly against her mug. "Besides the obvious appeal of being snowed in with our handsome concierge?" She winked at Adrian, who maintained his professional composure despite the teasing.

"I'm particularly interested in what happens behind closed doors," Lena said, leaning forward slightly. The question had been burning in her mind since Adrian's cryptic comments during their snow shoveling. "The rooms themselves—what makes them so special beyond their names and décor."

A charged silence fell over the group. Elena's eyebrow arched delicately while David and Michelle exchanged another of their meaningful glances. Adrian's posture stiffened almost imperceptibly beside her.

Elena was the first to break the silence, her rich laugh cutting through the tension. "Darling, if those walls could talk, they'd need their own podcast series." She took a deliberate sip of her coffee, eyes gleaming over the rim. "Each room is designed for... specific experiences. The Blush Desire Room, for instance, has the most magnificent ceiling mirrors I've ever seen."

"Elena," Adrian's voice carried a gentle warning.

"What? It's hardly a state secret that people come here for pleasure," Elena countered, waving a bejeweled hand dismissively. "The journalist already knows that much."

Lena seized the opening. "I'm curious about the custom furnishings Adrian mentioned. Each room supposedly has specialized equipment?"

Michelle's cheeks flushed a delicate pink. "The rooms are... accommodating to various interests." Her voice dropped to just above a whisper. "The Obsidian Discipline room has the most incredible suspension system built right into the ceiling. You'd never notice unless you knew what to look for."

David placed a steadying hand on his wife's knee. "Michelle."

"What? She's writing about the place. It's not like we're naming names," Michelle replied, though she did sit back in her chair, hands wrapped more tightly around her mug.

Lena tried another angle. "I've heard rumors about the fourth floor. What makes those rooms different?"

The temperature in the room seemed to drop several degrees. Elena's playful expression hardened into something more guarded, while David and Michelle suddenly found their coffee fascinating.

"The fourth floor is Echo's domain," Elena said finally, her tone deliberately light but lacking its earlier warmth. "I've never personally been invited to stay there."

"Nor have we," David added quickly. "Those rooms are... by special invitation only."

Adrian cleared his throat. "Echo maintains strict confidentiality about certain aspects of the Nest. It's part of what makes this place a sanctuary." His knee pressed gently against Lena's—a silent request to tread carefully.

Lena ignored the warning. "But surely as longtime guests, you must have heard stories?"

Elena's laugh held less warmth now. "Stories abound,

darling. Whether they're true is another matter entirely." She leaned forward, voice dropping conspiratorially. "They say the Writer's Muse on the fourth floor has walls that absorb sound so completely you could scream and no one would hear you. And the Spa of Sighs supposedly has heated floors and walls lined with natural salt that draws out impurities while you..." Elena trailed off, her eyes darting toward Adrian.

"While you relax," Adrian finished smoothly. "As I said, Elena loves to share the gossip, but that's all it is. The fourth floor is simply more exclusive."

"Not just exclusive," Elena corrected, leaning forward with renewed enthusiasm. "It's practically mythical. I've been coming here since opening night, and I've never set foot in any of the rooms on the fourth floor. None of us have." She gestured to include David and Michelle.

David absently touched his wedding band, twisting it as he spoke. "There's a special card scanner inside the elevator for the fourth floor. In all the times we've been here, I've never seen anyone actually use it."

"Oh, the stories I've heard though," Elena continued, her voice dropping to a dramatic whisper. "They say the Lodge Inferno room has walls that change color with body heat. And the Regal Chamber supposedly has a chair that..." She paused, glancing at Adrian with a mischievous smile. "Well, let's just say it extracts the truth in the most pleasurable way possible."

Lena watched Adrian's face carefully, noting how his expression remained neutral, though something flickered in his eyes—recognition, perhaps. He'd been there before, she realized. He knew exactly what was behind those fourth-floor doors.

"Elena has quite the imagination," Adrian said lightly, setting his mug down with a soft clink. "The fourth floor simply houses our most premium suites, along with Echo's private residence. The exclusivity fuels rumors, but that's the nature of sanctuary spaces—mystery enhances allure."

Michelle leaned forward, her auburn hair catching the light. "There was that famous actress last year—you know, the one who'd just come out in that interview—she stayed on the fourth floor. When she left, she looked... transformed. Glowing. Whatever happens up there, it's something special."

"Or maybe she just got a good night's sleep in our luxurious beds," Adrian countered, though his tone lacked conviction.

Lena's journalistic instincts tingled. There was definitely more to this story. "So no one gets invited to the fourth floor? Ever?"

"Echo extends invitations very selectively," Elena said, examining her perfectly manicured nails. "Usually to people in transition—not just gender transition, though that's common, but life transitions. Divorces, career changes, coming out later in life. People at crossroads." She looked up, fixing Lena with an intense gaze. "People who need to shed an old skin and discover what lies beneath."

The lobby fell silent save for the distant howl of wind outside. Lena felt Adrian shift beside her, his knee no longer pressing against hers. She missed the contact immediately.

Adrian abruptly stood, his chair scraping against the floor. "I believe that's enough for now." His voice carried the polite firmness of someone accustomed to ending conversations that ventured into forbidden territory. "Ms. Marquez has plenty of material for her article without delving into speculation about areas of the Nest that are off-limits."

Lena caught the shift in his tone immediately. The warm, playful Adrian from their snowy excursion had vanished, replaced by the consummate professional concierge. She reached for her recorder, clicking it off and tucking it back into her satchel.

"Thank you all for sharing your stories," she said, standing up to join Adrian. "You've given me some fantastic insights for my article."

Elena flashed a knowing smile as they walked across the lobby towards the elevator. "Don't be a stranger, darling," she called out to Lena. "I have many more tales to share when our strict concierge isn't around."

"I'm going to teach both David and Michelle how to dance," Elena added before they departed. "Feel free to join us."

"Thank you, I'll keep that in mind," Lena replied, pressing the elevator button.

The elevator doors opened with a soft ding, and Adrian gently guided Lena inside with a light touch on her back. As the doors shut, he let out a deep breath, his shoulders relaxing from their tense stance.

"I apologize for Elena," he said, running a hand through his hair. "She enjoys pushing boundaries, especially when it comes to the Nest's more... private aspects."

Lena leaned against the elevator wall, studying his face. "She certainly seems to know a lot for someone who claims never to have been to the fourth floor."

"Elena has been coming here since before we officially opened. She and Echo have history." Adrian's expression softened slightly. "She's harmless, really, just dramatic. Half of what she says is embellishment."

"And the other half?" Lena pressed, unable to resist.

The elevator slowed, stopping at the third floor. Adrian held the door open with one hand, gesturing for her to exit first. "The other half is exactly why Echo values privacy so highly." His eyes met hers, serious now. "Some things aren't meant for publication, Lena. Not everything that happens here belongs in your article."

Lena stepped into the hallway, the plush carpet muffling her footsteps. "You know my job is to find the story, right? The real one, not just the sanitized version you want me to tell."

Adrian followed her out, letting the elevator doors close behind them. "I'm not asking you to sanitize anything. I'm asking you to respect the boundaries that make this place special." He moved closer, his voice dropping lower. "The Heel's Nest isn't just a hotel with kinky furniture, Lena. It's a sanctuary where people can explore parts of themselves they keep hidden everywhere else."

Lena paused, struck by the sincerity in Adrian's voice. She had dealt with protective sources before, but Adrian's concern seemed to go beyond mere professional duty; he truly cared about safeguarding the Nest.

When they arrived at the door to her room, Adrian stopped. "I should probably check on a few things. But perhaps later this afternoon, before the club officially opens, we could visit The Glass Heel? Miko will be setting up the bar. She's quite the character—could add an interesting angle to your article."

"I'd love that," Lena replied, her writer's instincts immediately kicking in. "What time?"

"How about three? I'll come by your door," Adrian suggested.

Chapter 6

Heat Above the Club

As promised, at precisely three o'clock, Adrian's gentle knock echoed through Lena's room. She'd spent the intervening hours organizing her notes and photos, occasionally glancing out the window at the continuing snowfall. The city remained blanketed in white, with occasional flurries adding fresh layers to the already substantial accumulation.

The Glass Heel was eerily beautiful in its empty state. The space felt both larger and more intimate without the crowds—like a theater before the performance begins, full of potential energy waiting to be released.

Behind the bar, Miko moved with practiced precision, her jet-black bob swinging as she arranged bottles in perfectly straight lines. Her movements were economical, almost choreographed, each gesture flowing seamlessly into the next. She looked up as they approached, her dark eyes assessing them with quiet intelligence.

"The writer," she said, her voice carrying a hint of a Japanese accent. "Adrian mentioned you might stop by."

"Hope we're not interrupting," Lena said, sliding onto one of the high leather barstools.

"Not at all." Miko continued slicing limes into perfect wedges, her knife moving so quickly it became a silver blur. "I'm just prepping for tonight. We'll be quiet, but open. The regulars who live within walking distance will brave the snow."

Lena watched, fascinated by the bartender's methodical work. "Would it be okay if I asked you a few questions for my article? I'd love to include your perspective on The Heel."

"The Glass Heel," Miko corrected, her knife pausing mid-slice. "The Heel's Nest is upstairs. Different entities, same soul." She set down her knife and wiped her hands on a black cloth tucked into her waistband. "What do you want to know?"

"Everything," Lena admitted with a smile, pulling out her phone to take notes. "How you ended up here, your approach to bartending, what makes this place special from your perspective."

Miko considered this, her dark eyes studying Lena's face with quiet intensity. "Most journalists ask about celebrity gossip or what goes on in the rooms upstairs." She reached for a bottle of amber liquid, uncorked it, and poured a thimble-sized amount into a small glass. "Taste this."

Lena accepted the glass, bringing it to her nose first. The aroma was complex—honey, smoke, and something earthy she couldn't quite identify. She took a small sip, the liquid warming her tongue and throat with a gentle fire that bloomed rather than burned.

"Japanese whisky," Miko said, watching Lena's

reaction. "Aged in plum wine barrels. Notice how it changes as it sits on your tongue?"

Lena nodded, savoring the evolving flavors. "It starts sweet but finishes with something almost... mineral?"

A faint smile touched Miko's lips. "Good palate. That's the volcanic soil where the barley was grown." She took the glass back, her fingers brushing Lena's. "That's how I approach bartending—layers that reveal themselves slowly, a journey rather than just a destination."

"How did you learn that approach?" Lena asked, fingers moving across her phone screen to capture Miko's words.

"I trained in Tokyo under Hidetsugu Ueno-san at Bar High Five," Miko said, resuming her methodical slicing of citrus. "He taught me that a drink is not just alcohol—it's a moment captured in a glass." Her knife moved with surgical precision, each lime wedge identical to the last. "I spent five years learning to hand-carve ice, to measure without tools, to read a person's mood from how they sit on a barstool."

Adrian leaned against the bar, watching them with quiet interest. "Tell her about the memory thing," he suggested.

Miko's expression remained neutral, but something like pride flickered in her eyes. "I remember every drink I've ever made for a regular. Not just the ingredients—the occasion, their mood, who they were with." She arranged the lime wedges in a perfect fan pattern on a small plate. "It's not a party trick. It's respect for the moment we shared."

"That's incredible," Lena said, genuinely impressed. "Can you give me an example?"

Miko glanced at Adrian. "Two years ago, after Adrian's grandmother passed away, he came in looking like he'd lost his anchor. I made him a drink that wasn't on any menu—mezcal infused with cinnamon and orange peel, a splash of Pedro Ximénez sherry, and a single star anise floating on top." Her hands moved as she spoke, mimicking the preparation. "It was something his *abuela* might have recognized—familiar but elevated. He cried after the first sip."

Adrian cleared his throat, a faint flush creeping up his neck. "It tasted like her kitchen at Christmas."

Lena looked between them, caught by the genuine emotion in the exchange. She tapped a note into her phone, trying to capture the moment without breaking its spell.

"That's what I mean by intimacy," Miko continued, her fingers resuming their dance with the knife and limes. "A good bartender doesn't just serve alcohol. They serve moments, memories, comfort." She set the knife down and reached for a stack of cocktail napkins, aligning them with geometric precision at the corner of the bar. "What are you drinking tonight?"

Lena blinked, surprised by the sudden question. "Oh, I hadn't thought about it."

Miko's dark eyes studied her face for a moment, unreadable yet somehow seeing everything. "Something bright but grounding. Gin base, I think. You're someone who appreciates complexity but not pretension."

"That's... eerily accurate," Lena admitted, fascinated by the assessment.

"It's not magic," Miko said with a slight shrug. "It's observation. The way you hold yourself, how you listen rather than just wait to speak, the questions you choose." Her hands moved to a shelf of bitters, selecting three bottles with practiced efficiency. "People tell you who they are if you pay attention."

"Miko reads people better than anyone I've ever met," Adrian added, leaning forward slightly. "Remember that couple from Seattle last month? The woman who came in looking ready to murder someone?"

A rare smile flickered across Miko's face. "Her wife had forgotten their anniversary. She was contemplating divorce over a missed dinner reservation."

"Miko made her something with tequila and chile liqueur—"

"And grapefruit," Miko corrected. "The bitterness was essential."

"Right," Adrian continued. "By the time her wife showed up with flowers and apologies, the drink had cooled her temper just enough to listen."

"They left a two-hundred-dollar tip and a wedding photo," Miko added, reaching beneath the bar to produce a small, framed picture of two women in white dresses. "They come back every month now. I make them anniversary drinks."

Lena typed rapidly, trying to capture the essence of what she was witnessing. "So you're part mixologist, part therapist?"

"I prefer to think of it as reading between the lines," Miko said. "People come to bars for many reasons. The alcohol is rarely the primary one."

Lena nodded, watching as Miko's nimble fingers arranged a row of crystal mixing glasses, each catching the light differently. "So what brought you from Tokyo to Chicago? That's quite a journey."

Miko's hands paused, hovering over a bottle of bitters. Something shifted in her expression—a subtle tightening around the eyes that lasted only a moment before smoothing away.

"Initially, it was love," she remarked with a steady tone. "That didn't endure, but Chicago remained." She picked up a lemon, deftly slicing spirals of zest that twisted like yellow ribbons. "Echo gave me the creative freedom I couldn't find anywhere else. Julian Reyes, the other regular bartender, was the one who introduced me to her. In Tokyo, everything is governed by tradition—the exact angle of the ice, the precise number of stirs. Here, I could merge that precision with creativity."

"Miko's cocktail menu changes with the seasons," Adrian added, sliding onto the stool next to Lena. "The winter solstice menu is my favorite—all smoke and spice and warmth."

"The seasons give us natural rhythms to follow," Miko said. "In winter, people need warmth and comfort. In summer, brightness and escape." Her knife moved in a fluid arc, quartering an orange with mathematical precision. "A good bartender anticipates these needs."

Lena typed quickly, capturing Miko's philosophy. "You mentioned intimacy earlier. What did you mean by that?"

Miko set down her knife and looked directly at Lena, her dark eyes intent. "Think about it. A stranger tells me what they desire. I create something with my hands that they will take into their body. They trust me not to poison them." A faint smile curved her lips. "What could be more intimate than that?"

Lena felt heat rise to her cheeks at the unexpected framing. "I never thought of it that way."

"Most don't," Miko said, resuming her preparation. "They see transaction, not connection. But I know things about my regulars that their closest friends don't. I can tell when someone's relationship is ending before they can. I've witnessed first dates that became marriages and last conversations before divorces."

"She's not exaggerating," Adrian said. "Miko once refused to serve a regular his usual whiskey sour. Made him a non-alcoholic cocktail instead. Turned out he'd just started medication that would have interacted badly with alcohol. He hadn't told anyone, but she noticed the subtle tremor in his hands."

"You saved his life," Lena said, impressed.

Miko shrugged, the movement almost imperceptible. "I paid attention. That's all." She reached for a small notebook beneath the bar, its leather cover worn smooth with use. "I keep notes on every regular. Preferences, anniversaries, losses. I've found that most people are creatures of habit," Miko continued, her dark eyes glinting with amusement. "They order the same drink for years, convinced it's what they want, until someone shows them what they really need."

Lena nodded along to Miko's stories, her recorder capturing every word while her mind calculated angles. Each anecdote wasn't just interesting—it was currency, buying her the trust she'd need to ask about the Heel's Nest later.

The storm outside punctuated their conversation with distant thunder, while Lena's occasional laughter rang through the empty club. Amber light caught the bottles behind the bar, transforming them into jewels. Adrian's knee grazed hers as he shifted on his barstool, then retreated. She felt his glances like fingertips on her skin—brief touches that left warmth in their wake.

"I'd love to know more about the rooms in the Heel's Nest," Lena said, leaning in slightly. She maintained a casual tone, though her heart raced. This was the essence of what would make her article stand out—the hidden spaces that made The Heel famous in certain circles. "From a bartender's perspective, of course. You must hear quite a few stories from guests after their stays."

Miko's hands stilled on the cutting board. Her expression remained neutral, but something in her posture shifted, becoming more contained. She carefully set down the knife she'd been using and looked directly at Lena.

"I don't discuss the rooms," she said simply. Her voice was soft but firm, leaving no room for negotiation. "That's not my domain."

Lena tried again. "I'm not asking for specifics about guests, of course. Just your general impressions. The themes, perhaps? The special features Adrian mentioned earlier?"

"I mostly stay in The Glass Heel," Miko replied, her movements resuming but more measured now. "When I'm not behind this bar, I'm in the kitchen or the storage room. The Nest is..." She paused, selecting her words with precision. "A separate entity with its own rules."

"But surely you've been upstairs?" Lena pressed. The journalist in her couldn't let go, not when she sensed she was close to something substantial. "For cleaning, or deliveries?"

Miko's dark eyes flickered briefly to Adrian before returning to Lena. "The Heel's Nest has dedicated staff for those purposes." Her tone remained polite but had cooled noticeably. She reached for a bottle of bitters, adding precisely three drops to a small glass of clear liquid. "Would you like to try our signature winter aperitif? It's a blend of—"

"I'd really love to understand more about the connection between the club and the hotel," Lena interrupted, trying a different angle. "How they complement each other."

The silence that followed stretched uncomfortably. Miko's face revealed nothing, but her stillness spoke volumes. When she finally responded, her voice had dropped even lower.

"As I said, I don't discuss the rooms. It's not my place." She pushed the small glass toward Lena. "The aperitif has elderflower and a hint of star anise. Very refreshing."

Adrian cleared his throat. "Miko's being modest about her cocktail program," he said smoothly, shifting the conversation. "Did you know she creates custom drinks for every major performer who comes through? Tell Lena about that burlesque troupe from New Orleans last month."

Lena recognized the deflection but decided not to push further—for now. She'd hit a wall, and continuing to hammer at it would only close more doors. She took a sip of the aperitif instead, letting the complex flavors bloom across her tongue.

The hour melted away, each minute dissolving into the next like sugar into warm spirits. Miko's stories poured forth between tiny sample glasses that caught the light: the newlyweds who'd first locked eyes across her bar counter, the A-lister who shed her fame at the service entrance like an unwanted coat, the evening when technical failure had transformed into unexpected revelation. Through it all, Adrian's shoulder pressed against Lena's, his voice a warm counterpoint to Miko's measured cadence.

When Lena finally closed her notes app, her cheeks hurt from smiling.

"Thanks," she told Miko. "This was really helpful." Though it wasn't entirely true, she didn't want to upset Miko.

Miko nodded, cleaning her hands with a black cloth. "You ask insightful questions." She looked at Adrian, a silent understanding exchanged between them. "You might be beneficial for him."

Heat rushed to Lena's cheeks. Before she could respond, Adrian cleared his throat.

"We should head back upstairs," he said, his hand finding the small of her back. "Let Miko finish her prep in peace."

As they walked toward the exit, Lena felt his gaze on her profile. When she turned to meet it, his eyes held a warmth that made her breath catch.

"She likes you," he said quietly as they climbed the stairs. "That's rare."

The journey back to her room passed in comfortable silence, their shoulders occasionally brushing in the narrow hallway. As she entered the room, Lena felt the familiar weight of her camera in her hands, the smooth metal warming against her palms. Adrian followed, closing the door with a soft click that seemed to seal them into their own private world. Outside, the snow continued to fall in silent persistence, muffling the city beyond.

"I should probably get these photos organized," Lena said, moving toward the writing desk by the window. Her voice sounded different in her ears—softer, less certain than her usual professional tone.

Adrian nodded, but made no move to leave. Instead, he settled on the edge of the bed, his weight making the mattress dip slightly. "Mind if I stay a while? The lobby's too quiet, and Elena keeps trying to convince me to join her impromptu dance class in the lounge."

Lena laughed, the sound easing some of the tension that had been building between them since their walk in the snow. "By all means, hide out here. I promise not to make you plié."

She sat beside him on the bed, the mattress shifting to bring them closer, their shoulders brushing. The contact sent a small current through her arm, a warmth that had nothing to do with the room's temperature. The camera lay forgotten in her lap as silence settled between them—not uncomfortable, but weighted with unspoken possibilities.

"Thank you for introducing me to Miko," she said finally. "Her perspective adds so much depth to the article."

"She doesn't open up to many people," Adrian replied, his voice low and intimate in the quiet room. "You have a gift for making people comfortable. For seeing beyond the surface."

His praise made her feel a wave of delight unrelated to her professional achievements. "Journalists are trained to understand people," she remarked, brushing a lock of hair behind her ear. "Yet, it seems my abilities fell short with Miko and the enigma of the rooms at the Nest."

Adrian shifted his weight, causing the mattress to tilt slightly until their knees touched. The comment about Miko and the mysterious rooms hung in the air, deliberately unaddressed. "When you look at me," he murmured, his voice barely audible over the hum of the heating system, "is it always through a journalist's eyes?"

Something electric passed between them. Lena felt her heartbeat quicken as their gazes locked, his question hanging in the air like the last note of a song.

"I see you as more than just a story," she said softly, the admission slipping past her usual professional boundaries.

Adrian's eyes met hers, dark and steady. "I don't usually do this, you know."

"Do what?" she asked, though she already knew the answer.

"Let guests get close." His fingers traced an invisible pattern on the bedspread between them. "I keep my work and personal life separate. It's easier that way." He paused, and Lena watched the subtle shift in his expression—a vulnerability that hadn't been there before. "But you're... different."

Lena swallowed, her throat suddenly dry. "Different how?"

Adrian looked down at his hands, then back up at her. "I've shown you parts of The Glass Heel that I've never shown a journalist before. Told you stories I usually keep to myself." His voice dropped lower. "It's not just because of your article."

The admission hung in the air between them, changing the atmosphere of the room as surely as if someone had opened a window. Lena felt her pulse quicken, aware of the warmth radiating from Adrian's body so close to hers.

"I'm not just here for an article either," she admitted, her voice barely above a whisper. "Not anymore."

Adrian's hand moved to cover hers, his palm warm against her skin. The touch was gentle, almost tentative, as if he was giving her every chance to pull away. She didn't.

"I keep thinking about last night," he said. "Our dance. That kiss."

Lena nodded, her eyes meeting his. "Me too."

The space between them seemed charged with electricity, a tangible current that made her skin tingle with anticipation. Outside, the snow continued its silent descent, cocooning them in this moment, separate from the world beyond.

"This blizzard," Adrian murmured, his thumb tracing small circles on the back of her hand, "it's created this bubble where normal rules don't seem to apply."

"Is that what this is?" Lena asked. "A blizzard romance?"

Adrian's eyes darkened. "Is that all you want it to be?"

The question hung between them, weighted with possibility. Lena felt herself leaning closer, drawn by some invisible force that made resistance seem pointless.

"No," she whispered, the word barely audible even in the quiet room.

His free hand rose to gently cup her cheek, the touch so tender it sent a deep ache through her heart. Their eyes locked for a long, lingering moment, an unspoken exchange flowing silently between them like a river of understanding. Then Adrian closed the distance between them, his lips meeting hers in a kiss that began as soft as a whispered secret.

Unlike their first kiss—tentative and filled with unasked questions—this one quickly deepened with intensity. Lena's hand instinctively found its way to his chest, feeling the rapid drumming of his heartbeat beneath her palm. His arms wrapped around her, pulling her closer until she was nearly seated in his lap, the camera slipping from her grasp and landing on the floor with a gentle thud.

A searing heat bloomed between them, spreading through her body like a wildfire consuming a dry forest. Adrian's hands glided beneath her sweater, his fingers warm and firm against the small of her back. She gasped against his mouth at the intimate contact, her own hands diving into his hair, entwining with the silken strands.

Their kisses grew increasingly fervent, a hunger mounting with each passing heartbeat. Lena tugged at his sweater, suddenly overwhelmed by a desperate need to feel his skin against hers. Adrian paused just long enough to pull the garment over his head, revealing a landscape of smooth olive skin and the finely carved muscles of his chest and abdomen.

"You're beautiful," she breathed, her fingers tracing the contours of his shoulders.

Adrian's eyes, dark with desire, held hers as he reached for the hem of her sweater. "May I?"

Lena nodded, lifting her arms in a fluid arc to help him remove it. The cool air from the vents above raised delicate goosebumps across her collarbone and shoulders, tiny mountains that were quickly warmed by the heat of Adrian's amber-flecked gaze as it traveled over her with deliberate slowness. His eyes lingered on the contrast of black Chantilly lace against her skin, the delicate scalloped edge accentuating the swell of her breasts. His fingertips—calloused from years of hotel work yet impossibly gentle—traced the intricate pattern of the fabric, each point of contact sending electric shivers cascading down her spine like falling dominoes.

"You're sure about this?" he asked, his voice a rough velvet whisper, deeper than before, desire thickening his words while his espresso-dark eyes searched hers for the slightest hesitation.

In answer, Lena leaned forward, one hand cupping the sharp angle of his jaw, capturing his mouth with hers. This kiss tasted different—deeper, hungrier, flavored with cinnamon from his earlier tea and something uniquely him. It was a wordless, breathless yes that dissolved any remaining doubts between them like sugar in hot water. Heat sparked low in her belly, a molten pool spreading outward as Adrian's hands—warm and sure—moved to her back, his fingers finding the clasp of her bra with practiced ease, the metal hooks surrendering with a barely audible click.

The garment fell away, sliding down her arms like black water before landing forgotten on the rumpled duvet. Lena felt a heartbeat of vulnerability as Adrian's gaze traveled over her newly exposed skin, the winter light from the window painting half her body in cool blue shadows. But the reverence in his eyes—pupils dilated until only a thin ring of brown remained—banished any fleeting insecurity. His hands cupped the soft weight of her breasts, thumbs brushing across her rosy nipples in a touch so exquisitely gentle it pulled a surprised gasp from somewhere deep in her throat.

"Beautiful," he murmured against her skin as his lips traced a path down her neck.

Their movements took on an instinctive rhythm, each article of clothing discarded with increasing urgency. Adrian's dark-washed jeans joined her cream cashmere sweater on the mahogany floor, followed by mismatched argyle socks, her black lace demi-cup bra with its tiny satin bow, his charcoal boxers with the fraying elastic band, until nothing remained between them but heated skin—hers porcelain against his olive tone—and accelerated heartbeats that seemed to echo in the stillness of the room.

Lena's trembling fingers explored the defined planes of his chest, tracing the ridges of muscle beneath skin that felt like sun-warmed silk, while his calloused hands mapped the soft curves of her waist, the flare of her hips, discovering the sensitive hollow behind her knee that made her breath catch in her throat when he found it with his thumb. Each touch was a revelation written in goosebumps, each breathy sigh a confession neither had intended to make.

From below, the muffled thump of bass vibrated through the antique floorboards—Elena's impromptu salsa class in the club had apparently begun, the Latin rhythm pulsing up through the building's century-old bones like a second heartbeat that synchronized with their own racing pulses.

Adrian's full lips found the rosy peak of her breast, his tongue circling her nipple in slow, deliberate spirals that sent white-hot electricity arcing through her body like lightning across a summer sky. Lena's head fell back against the goose-down pillows, a soft, throaty moan escaping her parted lips as her fingers tangled in his thick raven hair, holding him closer to her flushed skin. The bass below intensified to a primal drumbeat, as if the music itself was responding to the heat building between their intertwined bodies.

"I want you," she whispered, the words both a confession and a plea.

Adrian raised his head, his eyes dark pools of desire as they met hers. "I've wanted you since you walked through that door," he admitted, voice rough with need.

He reached toward the polished wooden nightstand, his fingers sliding open the drawer with a soft scrape to retrieve a small foil packet, the promise of protection. Lena watched in silent admiration as the muscles in his back flexed and rippled like a well-tuned symphony with each movement, marveling at the effortless grace of his lean, athletic form. As he turned back to her, his gaze locked onto hers, she took the foil packet from his fingers, her eyes never wavering as she tore it open with a deliberate, confident motion.

The gentle touch of her hands as she carefully rolled the condom over him elicited a sharp, involuntary intake of breath from Adrian. His eyes remained fixed on hers, the connection between them deepening beyond the merely physical, a silent conversation of trust and desire as she guided him back to her embrace.

The first joining of their bodies was electric, drawing twin gasps from their lips, a harmony of surprise and longing. Lena arched beneath him, her fingers digging into the hard, sculpted muscles of his shoulders, their bodies beginning a slow, sensuous dance together. Their rhythm built gradually, like the gentle rise of a symphony, an exploration of each other's most intimate landscapes rather than a rushed crescendo, each thrust and response revealing new sensitivities, untapped pleasures.

Adrian's lips discovered the tender spot where her

neck met her shoulder, and Lena moaned softly, her hips rising to meet his with a natural, instinctive urgency. The deep, resonant bass from below vibrated through the floor, sending subtle tremors through the bed frame and into their intertwined forms—Elena's dance class in full swing now, the pulsating music setting a tempo that seemed perfectly synchronized with their movements, an unseen conductor guiding their shared rhythm.

Lena broke their rhythm, turning away from him with deliberate intent. She shifted onto her stomach, then rose to her knees, looking back over her shoulder with half-lidded eyes. The invitation in her gaze was unmistakable as she arched her back, presenting herself to him in a new way. Adrian's breath caught visibly in his throat, his hands trembling slightly as they found the curve of her hips. His fingertips pressed into her flesh, steadying them both as she reached back to guide him. Heat coursed through her body, anticipation mounting with each heartbeat.

"Lena," he whispered, her name a question on his lips.

She answered by reaching back, guiding his hand to the curve where her lower back met the swell of her buttocks. Her fingers pressed his there with deliberate intent, her meaning unmistakable. The bass notes thrummed through the mattress as she arched further, positioning herself in silent invitation, her body communicating what words couldn't in this moment of vulnerable trust.

Adrian shifted slightly, his questioning eyes meeting hers. Lena nodded, her breath catching as he reached for more lubricant. The cool gel warmed quickly between his fingers before he applied it with deliberate care. She felt the initial pressure as he eased himself against her—the exquisite tension of resistance followed by surrender as her body yielded to him. A gasp escaped her lips as he pressed deeper, filling her completely in this most intimate way. The sensation was overwhelming—pleasure radiating outward in waves that made her fingers clutch desperately at the sheets.

The tempo of the music below intensified to a frenetic crescendo, the pulsing Latin rhythm matching Adrian's measured thrusts as he withdrew almost completely before pressing forward again, stretching her in the most intimate way possible. Each careful movement sent contradictory sensations cascading through Lena's body—the initial resistance giving way to a pleasure so intense it bordered on pain, then transforming into something transcendent. She felt herself opening to him, accepting him deeper with each stroke. Adrian's breathing grew ragged against her neck, his control visibly fraying as her body gripped him, drawing him back each time he retreated, the slick heat between them building with every deliberate penetration.

"Don't stop," she breathed against his ear, her voice barely recognizable to her own ears.

Adrian shifted his rhythm, his movements becoming more insistent, the bed frame creaking softly beneath them with each deliberate thrust. His hand slid around the curve of her hip, fingers trailing over the dewy skin of her lower abdomen before finding its way between her legs. His fingers wrapped around her length—warm velvet over rigid steel—which had begun to swell and harden with each quickening pulse of arousal. The dual sensation of penetration and intimate touch made Lena gasp, her throat constricting around a sound that was half-plea, half-surrender as his firm grip stroked her from base to sensitive tip in perfect counterpoint to the deep, measured cadence of his thrusts.

"God," she moaned, her voice breaking as pleasure coursed through her from two directions at once.

Adrian's breath came hot against her ear as he established a steadier, more deliberate pace. His hand moved in long, measured strokes that matched the rhythm of his hips. Lena felt herself growing fully hard in his grasp, her body responding eagerly to his touch.

"Is this okay?" he whispered, his lips brushing against the sensitive skin below her ear.

"Yes," she managed, the word dissolving into another moan as he squeezed slightly at the upstroke. "Don't stop."

The bass from downstairs vibrated through the floor, setting a primal beat that Adrian followed instinctively. His thrusts deepened, finding a spot inside her that made stars burst behind her eyelids. The pleasure built in waves, each one higher than the last, until she was certain she couldn't bear any more. Adrian's hand moved faster, his grip firmer as his own control began to slip, his thrusts becoming more urgent.

"Lena," he gasped, his voice strained with the effort of holding back. "I'm close."

She reached back, her fingers digging into his thigh, urging him deeper. "Inside me," she whispered, the words barely audible over the pounding bass below. "Please."

His rhythm faltered, then accelerated as he drove into her with newfound urgency. His grip on her penis tightened, stroking in perfect counterpoint to his increasingly erratic thrusts. Lena felt the exact moment he surrendered—his body tensed, a deep groan tearing from his throat as he pressed impossibly deeper. She could feel the subtle pulse as he filled the latex barrier between them, the sensation triggering her own climax, pleasure exploding outward from her core in waves that left her gasping.

Her body convulsed in exquisite surrender as translucent nectar spilled over Adrian's skilled fingers, the warm wetness trailing down his knuckles and seeping into the sheets below. The climax bloomed through her differently now—where once it had been a sharp, localized explosion, hormone therapy had transformed it into a luscious, full-body awakening that radiated from her core to her fingertips. Each pulse of pleasure melted into the next like honey dissolving in hot tea, spreading through her limbs until even her toes curled in helpless rapture. She arched against him, her mouth forming a perfect O of wordless ecstasy as the sensation crested again and again, leaving her skin hypersensitive and glistening with a fine sheen of sweat.

They collapsed together onto the sheets, their breathing gradually slowing as the afterglow wrapped around them like a warm blanket. Adrian's arm draped over Lena's waist, his fingers tracing idle patterns on her skin. The distant thrum of music from below had shifted to something slower, more intimate—a perfect soundtrack to this moment of shared vulnerability.

Lena turned in his arms to face him, studying the way the fading afternoon light caught in his dark eyes, turning them to liquid amber. A small smile played at the corners of his mouth, softening his features.

"That was..." she began, searching for the right word.

"Unexpected?" Adrian offered, his voice a low rumble that she could feel against her chest where they touched.

She laughed softly. "I was going to say incredible, but unexpected works too."

His fingers continued their gentle exploration, trailing up her arm to her shoulder, then along the curve of her neck. "I've never done this before," he admitted.

"What, this specific activity?" Lena teased, her own hand coming to rest against his chest, feeling the steady rhythm of his heart beneath her palm.

Adrian's smile widened. "No, I mean... with a guest. I've always kept those boundaries clear." His expression grew more serious. "But there's something about you, Lena. From the moment you walked through that door with snow in your hair and that camera around your neck..."

Lena felt a smile bloom on her face at the warmth in Adrian's eyes. His words hung in the air between them, unfinished but full of meaning.

"From the moment I walked through that door...?" she prompted softly, her fingertips tracing small circles on his chest.

Adrian's hand found hers, their fingers intertwining. "I couldn't look away," he admitted. "There was something about you—this curiosity, this quiet confidence. I've watched hundreds of people walk through that door, but you..." He shook his head slightly, searching for words. "You saw things differently. Not just as a journalist looking for a story, but as someone seeking understanding."

The confession warmed her from the inside out, more intimate somehow than their physical connection had been. Lena shifted closer, her body fitting against his like puzzle pieces finding their match.

"I felt it too," she whispered. "That first day when you appeared from behind the reception desk. There was something familiar about you, like we'd met before in some other life."

Adrian's thumb traced her cheekbone, his touch feather-light. "I don't usually feel this comfortable with anyone. Especially not someone I've known for less than forty-eight hours."

"Is that all it's been?" Lena marveled, the realization striking her. "It feels like so much longer."

"The blizzard…" Adrian said, his gaze drifting to the window where only occasional snowflakes now drifted down, gentle remnants of last night's fury. "It changed everything."

"Will you stay with me tonight?" Lena asked, the words tumbling out before she could second-guess herself. Her heart quickened as Adrian's eyes widened slightly. "Not just for this," she added quickly, gesturing to their tangled limbs, "but to sleep. To wake up together."

The request hung in the air between them, vulnerable and honest. Adrian's expression softened as he considered her words, his fingers still idly tracing patterns on her skin.

"I shouldn't," he said finally, though his body remained pressed against hers. "I have the early shift tomorrow. And there's the professional boundary thing…"

Lena nodded, trying to mask the disappointment that settled in her chest. "I understand," she said, her voice steady despite the small ache blooming inside her.

Adrian's fingers paused their exploration, and he propped himself up on one elbow to look at her properly. The fading daylight caught the angles of his face, highlighting the slight furrow between his brows as he studied her.

"But I want to," he admitted, his voice dropping to just above a whisper. "That's the problem. I want to stay more than I should."

Lena reached up, her fingertips brushing against his cheek. "Then stay," she said simply. "The professional boundaries are already… well, thoroughly crossed." A small smile played at the corners of her mouth. "Besides, I've been told I don't hog the covers."

Adrian's smile bloomed slowly, his eyes crinkling at the corners as he gazed at her. "You make a compelling argument." He traced the curve of her shoulder with his fingertips, his touch light as a whisper. "And I've never been good at saying no to things I really want."

The confession hung in the air between them, simple and honest. Lena felt warmth spread through her chest, a quiet happiness that had nothing to do with physical desire and everything to do with the vulnerability in his eyes.

"I'll need to set an alarm," he added, reaching for his phone on the nightstand. "Early shift and all that."

"Responsible even when breaking the rules," Lena teased, watching as he programmed his alarm. The domesticity of the moment struck her—lying naked beside him while he performed such an ordinary task, as if they'd done this a hundred times before.

Adrian set his phone down and turned back to her. "Speaking of responsibility, I should probably shower before dinner." He pressed a kiss to her forehead, lingering there for a moment. "Care to join me? It's the environmentally conscious choice."

Lena laughed, the sound bubbling up from somewhere deep and genuine. "Is that the line you use on all your guests?"

"Only the ones who don't hog the covers," he replied, his smile turning mischievous as he slipped from the bed, extending his hand to her.

Chapter 7

The Thaw Approaches

Light spilled through the gauzy curtains, painting the rumpled sheets in a soft golden glow. Lena blinked awake, her muscles pleasantly sore from the night before, to find Adrian already propped against the headboard. The bedside clock showed 8:17—his alarm must have gone off ages ago while she'd slept straight through it. He watched her with a lazy smile that made her heart skip, looking far too alert for someone who should be equally exhausted.

"Morning," he murmured, his voice still rough with sleep. A silver tray sat on the bedside table, steam rising from a carafe of coffee and plates covered with silver domes.

"You brought breakfast?" Lena propped herself up on one elbow, the sheet sliding down to reveal her bare shoulder.

"Couldn't let you starve." Adrian's fingers traced a path along her collarbone, leaving a trail of warmth in their wake. "Though I considered keeping you hungry for... other reasons."

Heat bloomed across Lena's cheeks. Three days had passed since the storm had trapped them together, and the hours had melted into a haze of shared breaths, tangled limbs, and conversations that stretched until dawn. She'd learned the small scar near his temple came from falling off a bike at eight years old. He'd discovered her childhood dream of becoming a war photographer. Their bodies had mapped each other with increasing familiarity, finding the spots that made breath catch and backs arch.

Adrian poured coffee into two midnight-blue mugs, the rich aroma filling the space between them. His movements were unhurried, deliberate, as if they had all the time in the world. But when he handed her the steaming mug, his eyes flicked toward the window where sunlight streamed stronger than it had in days.

"The snow's starting to melt," he said, his tone carefully neutral.

Lena followed his gaze. Outside, icicles dripped from eaves, and patches of concrete had begun to emerge from beneath their white blanket. Reality was thawing its way back into their sanctuary.

"I suppose the city will be moving again soon," she replied, wrapping her fingers around the warm ceramic.

Adrian removed the silver domes to reveal plates of eggs benedict, the hollandaise sauce glistening in the morning light. "Miko insisted on making this herself. Said we needed the protein after our... exertions."

Lena laughed, grateful for the shift in mood. "Is there anything that woman doesn't know?"

"If there is, I've yet to discover it." Adrian handed her a plate, his fingers lingering against hers a moment longer than necessary. "She also sent up these."

He produced a small dish of chocolate-covered strawberries, the dark coating still glossy and perfect. Selecting one, he brought it to Lena's lips, his eyes never leaving hers as she took a bite. The chocolate shell cracked between her teeth, giving way to the sweet-tart flesh beneath. A drop of juice escaped the corner of her mouth, and Adrian caught it with his thumb, the touch sending a current down her spine.

"Delicious," she murmured, not meaning the strawberry at all.

Adrian smiled, a hint of wickedness in his eyes. "We have to keep our strength up." His voice dropped to a husky whisper. "I have plans for us later."

Lena felt heat spiral through her that had nothing to do with the coffee. She leaned forward, pressing a soft kiss to his lips, tasting chocolate and coffee and him. When she pulled back, his eyes had darkened, and she knew if she didn't redirect them, breakfast would be forgotten entirely.

"These eggs look amazing," she said, picking up her fork. "Miko really does think of everything."

Adrian's laugh was low and rich as he settled back against the headboard. "She's been teasing me mercilessly, you know. Says I'm walking around with a glow that's visible from space."

"And are you?" Lena asked, cutting into the perfectly poached egg, watching golden yolk spill across the English muffin.

"Absolutely," he admitted without hesitation. His knee nudged hers beneath the sheets. "Though I'm not the only one. Echo mentioned you looked particularly radiant yesterday."

Lena nearly choked on her bite. "She did not."

"She absolutely did. Said something about how certain rooms in the Nest tend to bring out people's inner light." His fingers trailed along her bare arm, leaving goosebumps in their wake. "Though I think that has more to do with the company than the room itself."

They ate in comfortable silence for a few moments, exchanging glances that held conversations of their own. Sunlight strengthened outside, highlighting the steady drip of melting icicles. A plow rumbled in the distance—the first Lena had heard since the storm began.

"They're saying the main roads will be clear by this afternoon," Adrian said, following her gaze to the window. Something flickered across his face—too quick to name, but Lena felt it like a shadow passing between them.

"I suppose normal life is waiting for us out there," she replied, trying to keep her tone light despite the sudden heaviness in her chest.

Adrian took her hand, his thumb tracing circles on her palm. "What does normal life look like for you, Lena Marquez? When you're not snowed in with overeager concierges?"

"Usually a lot more rushed," she admitted. "I'm typically juggling three assignments at once, living out of a suitcase, catching flights at ungodly hours."

"Always moving," he murmured.

"Always." She looked down at their joined hands. "My editor's already emailing about my next assignment. Seattle, then Vancouver."

Adrian nodded, his expression carefully neutral though his grip on her hand tightened slightly. "When?"

"The day after tomorrow," she said softly. "Assuming the airports are operating again."

"They will be." His certainty carried a note of resignation that made her heart twist.

Adrian gathered the empty plates, stacking them

neatly on the silver tray. The clink of porcelain against metal punctuated the silence that had settled between them. He'd dressed earlier, before she woke, his crisp shirt and tailored slacks a stark contrast to her nakedness beneath the sheets.

"I should see how everyone else is doing," he said, smoothing an invisible wrinkle from his sleeve. "Elena's called the front desk four times already about the roads. And now that things are thawing out, we'll have new arrivals to deal with."

Lena nodded, drawing the sheet higher over her chest. "Of course."

He leaned down to kiss her, his lips warm against hers. The kiss lingered, deepened, as if he was trying to memorize the feel of her. When he pulled away, his eyes held something that made her breath catch—a question, perhaps, or a goodbye not yet spoken.

"I'll come back later," he promised, his voice husky. His fingers brushed a strand of hair from her face with such tenderness that it made her chest ache. Then he was gone, the door closing softly behind him.

Lena sank back against the pillows, the warmth of his touch fading from her skin. The room felt suddenly larger, emptier without his presence. Outside, water dripped steadily from melting snow, a constant reminder that their bubble was dissolving.

She stared at the ceiling, tracing the ornate plasterwork with her eyes. What was she doing? This wasn't like her—falling into bed with a source, blurring the lines between professional and personal. And yet, the past three days had felt more real than anything she'd experienced in years.

Her phone buzzed on the nightstand. Another email from her editor: "Flight confirmed for Monday morning. Need the Heel piece by Tuesday night. Any juicy details?"

Lena set the phone down without replying. Monday morning. Less than twenty-four hours from now, she'd be on a plane heading west, this room and Adrian becoming just another memory, another place she'd passed through.

Was that all this was to him too? A beautiful distraction during an unexpected storm? The thought settled in her stomach like a cold stone. Men like Adrian—charming, attentive, devastatingly handsome—surely had women falling for them constantly. What made her any different from the countless guests who had passed through these doors before her?

She'd seen how naturally he moved through the social world of The Heel, how everyone from Miko to Elena responded to his easy charm. It was his job to make people feel special, seen. Perhaps she'd mistaken professional courtesy for something deeper.

Lena pressed her palms against her eyes, willing away the tightness in her chest. This was exactly why she kept moving, why she never stayed anywhere long enough to put down roots. Attachments meant vulnerability, and vulnerability meant the inevitable pain of separation.

Lena's suitcase lay half-packed in the corner, a visual reminder of her imminent departure. She'd tucked away her camera equipment and folded her professional clothes, leaving out only what she'd need for her final day.

Her thoughts circled back to Adrian. The way his eyes had dimmed slightly at the mention of Seattle. The careful neutrality of his expression. Was he simply being polite? A consummate professional managing a guest's departure?

Lena rolled onto her side, pulling the sheets tighter around her naked body. The space beside her still held the impression of his weight, the pillow carrying the faint scent of his cologne. Three days. That's all this had been—three days of unexpected intimacy created by extraordinary circumstances.

The bubble of the blizzard had made everything feel heightened, intensified. Cut off from the world, they'd connected in ways that might never have happened otherwise. But now the snow was melting, reality seeping back in with each drip from the eaves.

She stared at the window, watching a droplet trace its way down the glass. How many other guests had Adrian charmed during storms? How many had left thinking they'd found something special, only to become another anecdote, another memory in the long history of The Heel's Nest?

The thought made her stomach clench. She'd let herself forget the temporary nature of their connection. She was just passing through—as always. Her life was built on movement, on never staying still long enough for roots to form. That was the price of her freedom, the cost of the career she'd chosen.

And Adrian belonged here, as much a fixture of The Heel as Echo or the memorial wall. His life was built around welcoming people, making them feel special, and then watching them leave.

Lena pressed her face into the pillow, inhaling his lingering scent. She'd been foolish to think this could be anything more than what it was—a beautiful, fleeting connection, a warm shelter in the middle of a storm. Tomorrow or the next day, she'd walk out those doors and become just another guest who had passed through. Another name Adrian would eventually struggle to recall when reminiscing about memorable stays.

Her phone buzzed again—her editor, no doubt, impatient for updates on the article. Lena ignored it. She'd need to focus soon, to transform these intimate days into professional prose, to package their connection into something her readers could consume with their morning coffee.

The thought left a bitter taste in her mouth.

A soft knock at the door pulled her from her spiraling thoughts. Lena sat up, clutching the sheet to her chest. "Yes?"

"It's Echo," came the melodious voice from the hallway. "May I have a word, Ms. Marquez?"

Lena scrambled from the bed, grabbing her robe from the floor where it had been discarded the night before. "Just a moment," she called, hastily tying the sash and running fingers through her tangled hair.

Lena opened the door, finding Echo standing there in a deep burgundy dress that seemed to absorb the hallway light. The woman's presence immediately transformed the doorway, making the ordinary threshold feel suddenly significant, as if it had become a boundary between worlds rather than mere rooms.

"Good morning, Ms. Marquez," Echo said, her near-silver eyes taking in Lena's disheveled appearance with a subtle glance that missed nothing. "I hope I'm not interrupting your morning."

"Not at all," Lena replied, tightening the belt of her robe. "Please, come in."

Echo glided into the room, her movements fluid and deliberate. She paused near the window, observing the melting snow outside with a contemplative expression.

"I see Adrian has been taking good care of you during your stay," she remarked, her silver gaze lingering on the rumpled sheets and twin depressions in the pillows. "Has everything been to your satisfaction?"

Lena felt heat rise to her cheeks. "Yes, Adrian has been... exceptionally attentive."

"I'm glad to hear it." Echo's lips curved into a knowing smile. "The Heel's Nest prides itself on personalized service."

The way she emphasized "personalized" made Lena's blush deepen. She cleared her throat, recognizing an opportunity she couldn't let pass.

"Actually, I was hoping to speak with you before I leave," Lena said, gesturing toward her notebook on the nightstand. "My article would benefit greatly from your perspective as the creator of this place. Would you be willing to be interviewed?"

Echo regarded her for a long moment, her expression unreadable. Then she nodded, a faint smile playing at the corners of her red lips.

"I suppose it's only fair," she said, settling gracefully into the armchair by the window. "You've experienced our hospitality so... thoroughly."

Lena grabbed her notebook and pen, trying to shift mentally from the vulnerable woman who'd been wallowing in bed to the professional journalist with a deadline. She perched on the edge of the mattress, keeping the sheet wrapped around her legs.

"The Heel's Nest is unlike any hotel I've ever visited," Lena began, pen poised over paper. "What was your vision when you created it?"

Echo's elegant fingers traced the arm of the chair as she considered the question. "I designed The Heel's Nest to serve dual purposes," she said, her voice measured and melodic. "It is both sanctuary and stage—a place where people can feel protected enough to explore aspects of themselves they keep hidden elsewhere."

Lena scribbled notes, captivated by Echo's precise articulation. "And the themed rooms? They seem to each tell a different story."

"Absolutely," Echo replied as she crossed her legs, the fabric of her dress swishing softly. "The rooms on the second floor are all about approachability, fantasy roleplay, and playful seduction, whereas those on the third floor emphasize darkness, intensity, and avant-garde erotic experiences."

"And the fourth floor?" Lena asked, her journalistic instinct pushing her forward despite the slight tightening of Echo's expression.

Echo studied her for a moment, silver eyes unblinking. "The fourth floor requires a higher level of discretion. The experiences there are... more profound."

Lena leaned forward. "In what way?"

"When I created The Heel's Nest," Echo said, smoothly redirecting, "I envisioned a space where transformation wasn't just possible, but inevitable. The fourth floor embodies that vision in its purest form."

Lena's pulse quickened. "Could you elaborate on what makes the fourth floor different? Is it the clientele, the activities, or something else entirely?"

Echo's expression sharpened ever so slightly, her silver eyes cooling by degrees. The temperature in the room seemed to drop with her gaze.

"I cannot give you details," she said, her melodic voice carrying a new edge of finality. "But I will let you see the hallway."

Lena blinked, surprised by the unexpected offer. "Really?"

"Consider it a professional courtesy." Echo rose in one fluid motion, her burgundy dress settling around her like liquid shadow. "Get dressed. I'll wait in the hallway."

Heart racing, Lena fumbled with the buttons of her cable-knit sweater, the wool catching on her still-damp skin. She yanked faded jeans over her hips, not bothering with socks as she shoved bare feet into worn leather boots.

Her notebook—dog-eared at the corners, its spine cracked from overuse—went into her back pocket while her phone, screen smudged with fingerprints, disappeared into her palm. The promise of exclusive access thrummed in her veins like electricity, a journalist's high more potent than caffeine.

When she joined Echo in the corridor, the older woman stood motionless, her burgundy dress pooling around her ankles like spilled wine. The hallway's amber sconces caught the silver threads woven through Echo's dark hair, creating a halo effect that made her seem both ancient and ageless. Without acknowledgment, Echo pivoted with balletic precision and glided toward the elevator, her heels somehow absorbing all sound against the midnight-blue carpet patterned with golden constellations.

In the elevator's polished confines, Echo's reflection multiplied in the mirrored walls as she reached into some hidden pocket within the folds of her dress. The keycard she produced was obsidian black with a matte finish that absorbed light rather than reflected it—a stark modern intrusion against the hotel's carefully cultivated antiquity. Her crimson-lacquered nail tapped once against the card before she passed it over a nearly invisible sensor, its blue light briefly illuminating the underside of her jaw.

"The fourth floor requires a higher level of discretion," she explained, her tone carrying both finality and invitation as the elevator hummed to life.

Lena watched the floor numbers illuminate in sequence: L... 2... 3... 4. The elevator slowed to a stop, and for a heartbeat, Lena held her breath, unsure what to expect when the doors parted.

The hallway that greeted her was nothing like the others. Where the second and third floors featured warm woods and amber lighting, this corridor was a study in crimson and shadow. Erotic oil paintings hung in heavy frames of blood-red wood, their figures rendered in strokes that were equal parts intimate and mythic. The hardwood floors beneath their feet were painted the same blood-red, polished to a mirror sheen that reflected the warm glow of low sconces.

The fourth-floor hallway drew Lena forward as if she were stepping into the unlit backstage of a high-stakes production, each detail calibrated to create a sense of both awe and unease. Five massive doors lined the corridor, each one a statement. 401: The Spa of Sighs, the words inlaid in mother-of-pearl, the curves of the font evoking a sinuous, underwater languor. Next, 402: The Riviera Suite, letters hand-painted in electric blue against glossy white, conjuring the crisp bite of sea air and sun-drunk decadence. 403: The Writer's Muse announced itself in a spidery, looping script, each letter a miniature knot of hunger and longing. 404: The Regal Chamber, old gold leaf pressed into deep mahogany, the font so severe it was almost a dare. Last, 405: The Lodge Inferno, the words gouged into scorched wood, edges burned and still faintly aromatic, as if the door had just come from the flames.

Lena could picture the guests drifting down this hallway at midnight, each drawn to whichever name called out to the animal in their chest. There was nothing playful about these doors. They didn't promise only pleasure; they hinted at friction and consequence, at the possibility that you might leave the room changed—or not leave at all. She wondered which she would want for herself.

Directly opposite the elevator, Echo stopped before the only unmarked door in the hallway. Its blankness was more striking than the brazen signage surrounding it. The wood was a matte black, indistinguishable from the shadows in the corners, the frame trimmed with a subtle line of silver only visible when the light hit just so. There was no knob, no visible means of entry. Echo placed her palm flat against the center, as though greeting an old friend.

"This is my suite," she said quietly. "No one enters unless I open it first."

Lena's throat felt tight. "Have you ever invited anyone inside?"

Echo's near-silver eyes slid over Lena, briefly considering her. "On rare occasions. Only when the guest has earned it."

It felt like a challenge, and Lena filed it away with a pulse of anxious curiosity.

They continued down the corridor, Echo pausing at the door of 404: The Regal Chamber. She traced the gold-leafed numerals with her fingertip. "Each room is more than a theme. It's a crucible," she said. "Designed not just to contain, but to catalyze. Clients request a chamber. The walls, the furnishings, the scents—they're all tailored to encourage a particular form of surrender."

Echo reached for the next door, The Lodge Inferno, her nails catching briefly on the charred wood. "And transformation always requires heat."

Lena hovered between fascination and fear. "What actually happens in these rooms?"

Echo smiled, teeth white and deliberate. "That's for the walls to remember and the guests to forget, if they choose."

A shudder passed through Lena. She imagined the human stories that had played out behind these doors: the confessions and humiliations, the consensual deconstructions and careful rebuildings. She thought of herself lying awake the night before, craving a kind of vulnerability she'd never had the courage to name.

Echo paused at the unmarked door once more,

resting her hand on the blank wood. "These rooms," she said again, softer this time, "are not for comfort or titillation. They're for those who want to risk something essential. Who understand that pleasure, by itself, is just a rehearsal for the real thing."

Lena met her gaze, searching for any hint of insincerity. There was none.

"Metamorphosis," Echo said, as if the word itself were a prayer. "It's never safe. Sometimes you don't survive it."

Lena swallowed, stunned by the gravity in Echo's voice—the way she spoke as if this were an article of faith. "Is that what happened to you?"

Echo's smile was small and unguarded. "I'm still in rehearsal, Ms. Marquez. As are we all."

Something in Lena loosened at that. She felt, for the first time in weeks, the faintest hope that transformation could be voluntary—that you could choose to become more than you were, if you dared to submit to the process.

Echo turned away from the doors, leading Lena back toward the elevator. "Would you like to see my favorite painting?" she asked, her tone suddenly lighter, playful.

Lena nodded, eager for the reprieve.

Echo stopped before a canvas hanging just outside her private suite. It was a study in chiaroscuro: a woman perched on a velvet throne, one breast artfully exposed, her legs draped in a way that was both inviting and imperious. A glass slipper dangled from her foot, impossibly delicate, catching the candlelight like a prism. Shadows clustered at the throne's base—lovers, admirers, or perhaps former versions of herself, all blurred and desperate to touch the hem of her garment.

Lena stared, transfixed. The painting's subject looked out at the viewer with a gaze that was both accusation and seduction.

Echo's voice floated beside her: "She reminds me of what it means to rule yourself. Even when others believe they own you."

Lena blinked, feeling the room settle around her. "She looks like you."

Echo laughed, a sound rich and rare. "In the right light, she does."

The two women stood before the painting for a long moment, the silence between them charged with possibility.

"Thank you for showing me this," Lena said quietly.

Echo smiled. "You're welcome. Not everyone wants to see what's behind the doors."

As she entered the elevator, Lena felt changed—not entirely, but imperceptibly, in the way a deep cut changes the texture of the skin after it heals. She wondered what story she would write about this place, and if it would betray the intimacy Echo had let her glimpse.

Before Lena could press the elevator button, Echo placed two fingers lightly on her wrist. "The doors that matter, Ms. Marquez," she said, her voice barely above a whisper, "are the ones we're most afraid to open."

The elevator descended with a silken hum, Echo's final words reverberating in Lena's mind like the lingering note of a struck bell. Doors we're afraid to open. Her stomach tightened with a strange mix of exhilaration and dread, a physical sensation like standing at the edge of a precipice. What had she just witnessed? The fourth floor with its scorched wood and mother-of-pearl inlays felt like stepping into another dimension—one where fantasy and reality blurred into something darker, more primal, where even the air tasted different, heavy with secrets and possibility.

When the brushed steel doors slid open onto the lobby with a soft pneumatic sigh, Lena blinked against the sudden brightness. Winter daylight streamed through the floor-to-ceiling windows, harsh and unforgiving after the crimson-tinged shadows above. She stepped out onto cool marble, her heels clicking softly, still half-lost in thoughts of velvet thrones and glass slippers that caught light like trapped stars.

Adrian stood near the reception desk, his tall frame angled toward the muscular security guard she recognized as Darius. They bent over a clipboard, checking what looked like a delivery manifest. Adrian wore dark jeans and a charcoal sweater that made his olive skin glow, his hair slightly mussed as if he'd been running his hands through it.

"The champagne delivery needs to go directly to cold storage," Adrian was saying. "And make sure the florist knows—"

He glanced up, his sentence trailing off as his eyes found hers across the lobby. Something shifted in his expression—a softening, a recognition that made her chest tighten. Without finishing his thought, he murmured something to Darius and handed over the clipboard.

Lena moved toward the window, drawn by the sight of melting snow dripping from the eaves. The sun had broken through the clouds, transforming ice crystals into prisms that scattered tiny rainbows across the glass. She heard Adrian's footsteps approaching, measured and deliberate on the marble floor.

"Hey," he said, his voice low as he came to stand beside her. "I see Echo gave you the tour."

Lena nodded, not quite trusting her voice. The silence between them felt weighted, charged with all the things they weren't saying—desires still warm from Echo's tour, questions about what might happen after tomorrow's flight. Outside, a city plow rumbled past, its massive orange blade scraping against asphalt with a sound like distant thunder, pushing dirty slush into ridged banks that glistened wetly in the winter light. Flecks of snow clung stubbornly to the window's edge, melting into teardrops that traced slow paths down the glass.

"Your flight's tomorrow," Adrian said finally. Not a question—a statement of fact that hung in the air between them.

"Early morning," she confirmed, watching another icicle surrender to the sun, water droplets catching the light as they fell. "Assuming the runways are clear."

Adrian shifted beside her, close enough that she could feel the warmth radiating from his body, yet not touching. "Listen, Lena," he began, then paused, searching for words. "I need to tell you something."

She turned to face him, struck again by how easily she found his eyes in any room, how natural it felt to be in his orbit. The lobby around them—with its polished surfaces and perfect lighting—suddenly seemed too public for whatever was coming.

"This isn't normal for me," Adrian said, his voice dropping lower. "I've never crossed this line before—inviting a guest into my personal life, blurring professional boundaries like this." His eyes held hers, unguarded and earnest. "In five years at The Nest, I've never once..." He trailed off, searching for words.

"Never once what?" Lena asked, her heart beating faster despite her attempt to remain composed.

"Never once wanted someone to stay." The confession hung between them, raw and honest. "There's something about you, Lena. Something that feels..." He paused, running his hand through his hair again. "Different. Important."

Lena's chest tightened. She'd been so certain this was just a blizzard romance, a beautiful distraction during exceptional circumstances. To hear him echo her own unspoken feelings made her dizzy with hope and terror in equal measure.

"I know you're leaving tomorrow," he continued. "I know your life is built around constant movement. Mine is rooted here." His fingers reached for hers, a tentative touch that sent warmth spiraling up her arm. "But I don't want this to be just some fling that ends when the snow melts. I can't pretend that's all it is for me."

The sunlight caught his profile, highlighting the strong line of his jaw, the vulnerability in his eyes. Lena swallowed hard, feeling as though she stood at a precipice.

"I feel it too," she admitted, her voice barely above a whisper. "This connection. But it terrifies me." Her fingers tightened around his. "My whole life is about moving on, never staying in one place long enough to..." She couldn't finish the thought.

"Long enough to get hurt," he finished for her.

Lena nodded, a lump forming in her throat. "My career takes me everywhere and nowhere. Three days here, a week there. I don't know how to want more than that. I don't know if I can."

Adrian's thumb traced slow circles on her palm. "I'm not asking you to give up your career or your freedom. I wouldn't want that." His eyes held hers, steady and sure. "But maybe there's a middle ground. Maybe we could find a way to build something that bends rather than breaks."

"What would that even look like?" Lena asked, though her mind was already racing ahead, imagining possibilities she'd never allowed herself to consider before.

"I don't know yet," Adrian admitted. "But I'd like the chance to figure it out. With you."

The honesty in his voice made her chest ache. This wasn't a practiced line from a charming concierge; this was Adrian—uncertain, hopeful, laying his heart bare in the middle of the lobby where anyone might see.

"I'm afraid," Lena whispered, the admission costing her more than she'd expected. "Afraid of wanting something I might not be able to have."

Adrian took a deep breath. "I know. I'm scared too." He reached up, his fingertips lightly brushing her cheek. "But what scares me more is letting you walk away tomorrow without saying any of this. Without at least trying."

Lena leaned into his touch, closing her eyes briefly. When she opened them, she saw the same mixture of hope and fear she felt mirrored in his gaze.

"I don't do this either," she admitted. "I don't fall for the people I write about. I keep moving, keep working. It's safer that way."

"And now?"

"Now I don't know what I want more—to run or to stay." The confession left her feeling exposed, vulnerable in a way that made her pulse quicken.

Adrian's hand dropped from her face, finding hers again. His thumb traced the lines of her palm as if reading her future there.

"What if," he said slowly, "instead of trying to figure everything out right now, we just focus on tonight? One last night without overthinking or doubting or worrying about tomorrow's flight."

Lena felt something loosen in her chest—not a solution, but a reprieve. "Just be present," she murmured. "No expectations beyond this moment."

"Exactly." His eyes held hers, warm and steady. "We

have tonight. Let's make it count."

The simplicity of it—the permission to just exist in this connection without demanding answers about what came next—felt like stepping out of a too-tight garment. Lena nodded, a small smile forming.

"I'd like that," she said softly. "One perfect night."

Adrian's answering smile made her heart skip. "I need to finish up some things at the desk, but I'll come to your room at eight?" His fingers tightened briefly around hers. "I have something special planned."

"Eight it is," she agreed, suddenly eager for the evening to arrive.

They parted reluctantly, his hand lingering against hers until the last possible moment. As Lena walked toward the elevator, she felt his gaze following her, warm against her back like sunlight. The weight that had settled in her chest when she'd woken to melting snow had lifted, replaced by a tremulous anticipation.

One perfect night. No promises beyond that, no expectations that might shatter in the cold light of tomorrow's departure. Just this—whatever this was between them—honored and embraced for exactly what it was.

The elevator doors closed, and Lena leaned against the mirrored wall, her reflection showing flushed cheeks and bright eyes. She looked... alive. Present in a way she hadn't been in longer than she could remember. Always moving toward the next assignment, the next story, never fully inhabiting any single moment.

But tonight would be different. Tonight she would be nowhere but here, with no one but him.

Chapter 8

The Last Night in 312

The knock came at precisely eight o'clock, three soft raps that made Lena's heart leap into her throat. She smoothed her hands down the front of her dress—a deep burgundy number she'd packed on a whim—and took one last glance in the mirror before crossing to the door.

Adrian stood in the hallway, tall and elegant in a charcoal suit that fit him like a second skin. His dark hair was swept back, revealing the strong line of his jaw, and when his eyes met hers, Lena felt a flutter low in her belly.

"You look stunning," he said, his voice carrying that perfect blend of reverence and desire that made her skin warm. He extended his hand, a simple gesture that somehow felt weighted with significance. "Ready?"

Lena nodded, slipping her fingers into his. The contact sent a familiar current up her arm. "Lead the way."

Instead of taking the main elevator, Adrian guided

her toward the hidden staircase they'd discovered days earlier. His hand rested lightly at the small of her back, warm through the thin fabric of her dress. The stairs descended in a graceful spiral, each step illuminating with that same amber glow as they approached, then fading once they passed.

"The Glass Heel is different at night," Adrian murmured as they reached the landing. "It's like watching a butterfly emerge from its chrysalis."

He pushed open the heavy door, and sound washed over them—the low thrum of bass, the clink of glasses, murmured conversations blending into a texture as rich as velvet. Lena stepped through the doorway and felt her breath catch.

The club she'd seen earlier that day had transformed. Soft blue light pulsed across the dance floor in hypnotic waves, making the polished wood seem like the surface of some otherworldly ocean. Mirrors caught and multiplied the colored lights, creating the illusion of infinite space. The air tasted of anticipation, spiced with perfume and the faint sweetness of top-shelf liquor.

In the DJ booth, a woman with rich mahogany skin and a high, voluminous puff of hair moved with fluid grace, her hands dancing over equipment with practiced precision. Her head bobbed slightly to the rhythm she was creating, a smile playing at the corners of her mouth as she layered sound upon sound.

"That's Heather," Adrian said, his lips close to Lena's ear. "She's been with Echo since opening night. Nobody reads a room like she does."

Across the floor, the bar glowed golden, a beacon in the blue-tinged darkness. Behind it, Miko moved with the same elegant efficiency Lena had observed earlier, her sleek bob swinging as she reached for bottles without needing to look at the labels. Beside her, a tall man with dark curls pulled back in a short ponytail worked in perfect tandem, their movements so synchronized they seemed to be performing a dance they'd rehearsed.

"Let me show you something special," Adrian said, his hand sliding to her waist as he guided her away from the stairs. Instead of descending to the dance floor, he led her along a narrow walkway that hugged the perimeter of the club. The pathway curved upward, following the contour of the wall until they reached a secluded alcove overlooking the entire space.

"Echo's private booth," he explained, gesturing to the plush velvet seating arranged in a half-moon. "The best view in the house."

Lena stepped into the space, immediately drawn to the railing that separated the booth from the open air above the club. From this vantage point, the entire Glass Heel spread beneath her like a living painting. The perspective transformed everything—what had seemed intimate at ground level now revealed itself as an intricate composition of light and movement.

"This is incredible," she breathed, leaning slightly forward.

Adrian stood beside her, close enough that she could feel the warmth radiating from his body. "Echo designed it this way. She says you can't truly understand the heart of a place until you've seen it from above."

Lena watched as the first guests filtered in through the main entrance, their movements hesitant at first, then growing more confident as the space embraced them. Near the door, Echo stood in a silver dress that caught the light like mercury, greeting each arrival with a touch to the elbow or a whispered word that seemed to instantly relax them. A couple lingered near the bar, the taller woman's hand resting protectively at the small of her partner's back as Echo approached them with a familiar smile. A group of friends claimed a corner table, their laughter floating upward like bubbles in champagne after Echo had personally escorted them to their seats.

"Come, sit," Adrian said, guiding her to the curved seating. The velvet was butter-soft beneath her fingers, the deep purple almost black in the dim lighting.

As they settled into the booth, Lena felt the bass notes from below vibrate subtly through the floor and up into her body. The sensation was strangely intimate, as if the club's pulse had synchronized with her own. She leaned back, letting the music wash over her.

"The regulars arrive first," Adrian explained, his voice low in her ear. "They know to come early, before the energy shifts."

True to his words, Lena watched as familiar faces appeared below. Elena Rodriguez made her entrance with theatrical timing, pausing in the doorway just long enough for heads to turn before gliding toward her usual spot at the bar. Echo caught Elena's eye across the room and offered a small, knowing smile that Elena returned with a slight tilt of her chin. David and Michelle followed shortly after, their hands linked as they navigated to a small table near the dance floor.

The bar glowed golden beneath Miko's expert touch, bottles illuminated from below like precious artifacts. Julian moved with equal precision beside her, the two of them creating a synchronized ballet of service that was mesmerizing to watch.

"It's like watching a ceremony," Lena murmured, transfixed by the scene unfolding below.

Adrian nodded, his shoulder pressing against hers. "Every night has its own rhythm, its own story. But the beginning is always the same—this slow build, this gathering of energy."

The dance floor, still mostly empty, gleamed under the shifting lights, but Lena's attention kept drifting to Echo. From this vantage point, she could observe every subtle move the club owner made. Echo glided between guests with effortless precision, like a conductor leading an orchestra no one else could hear.

When a young woman in a blue sequined top hesitated at the entrance, Echo materialized beside her, leaning in to whisper something that transformed the newcomer's nervous expression into a smile. With the lightest touch to her elbow, Echo guided her toward a small table where three others waited, their faces lighting up at the arrival. The connection forged in seconds, the anxiety dissolved with a few words – it was masterful.

"She sees everything, doesn't she?" Lena murmured, leaning slightly forward.

Adrian's voice was warm in her ear. "Echo has this theory that nightlife is about energy transfer. She says the wrong word at the wrong moment can collapse an entire evening."

Below, Echo paused at the bar, accepting a glass of deep red wine from Miko with a nod of thanks. She took a single sip before setting it down to embrace a pair of regulars who'd just arrived – an older couple whose faces transformed with pleasure at her recognition. The wine sat untouched for minutes as Echo focused entirely on them, her attention absolute until she'd guided them to their favorite corner.

Lena watched, fascinated, as Echo moved to the edge of the dance floor where a tall man in an impeccably tailored suit stood alone, his posture rigid with discomfort. Echo approached him not head-on but at an angle, her body language open yet respectful of his space. Within moments, his shoulders relaxed, and something that might have been a laugh escaped him. Echo signaled to Julian with the slightest tilt of her head, and seconds later, a drink appeared in the man's hand – something amber in a heavy crystal glass.

"It's like watching someone speak a language I can barely comprehend," Lena said.

"She reads micro-expressions better than anyone I've ever met," Adrian replied. "Notice how she never stays too long with any one person? She's maintaining the flow, making sure no single interaction disrupts the larger pattern."

The club had filled steadily, the energy building like a tide. Echo now sat at her corner seat at the bar, that same glass of wine finally in her hand. From there, she had a clear view of every entrance and exit, every shadowed corner. Though she appeared relaxed, Lena noticed how Echo's eyes never stopped moving, cataloging a thousand tiny interactions.

When a sharp laugh cut through the music – too loud, too harsh – Echo's gaze flicked immediately to its source. A man at the bar was leaning too close to a woman whose smile had frozen in place. Before Lena could even process what was happening, Echo had set down her glass and crossed the floor. Her approach was casual, unhurried, yet somehow she inserted herself smoothly between them, a smile that illuminated her face but never quite reached her eyes. Within moments, the man had backed away, his demeanor shifting from predatory to almost apologetic.

"She's like a chess master," Adrian said, his admiration evident. "Always three moves ahead."

Lena was about to respond when movement in her peripheral vision caught her attention. Echo was no longer at the bar. Instead, she was ascending the stairs to the VIP booth, her silver dress catching fragments of colored light from below. She moved with fluid grace, each step deliberate yet effortless, as if gravity affected her differently than everyone else.

Echo slipped into the booth beside them, the velvet cushions barely whispering beneath her weight. Up close, Lena could see the intricate details of her appearance—the subtle silver threading woven through her raven-black hair, the precise arch of her brows, the luminous quality of her skin that seemed to glow from within.

"I hope you're enjoying the view," Echo said, her voice a melodic contralto that somehow cut through the music without being raised. "It's where I come to take the pulse of the evening."

"It's incredible," Lena replied, suddenly aware of how close they were sitting, the three of them forming an intimate triangle in the plush booth. "I've been watching you work the room. It's like... choreography."

Echo's lips curved into a smile that transformed her face, softening the regal angles into something warmer, more approachable. "That's exactly what it is. A dance where everyone has a part, whether they realize it or not."

She turned her gaze to the club below, her near-silver eyes reflecting the dance of colored lights. "What you're seeing is connection in its purest form. Everyone who walks through those doors is searching for something—acceptance, desire, release, or simply the comfort of being seen." Echo's voice dropped lower, becoming almost hypnotic in its cadence. "My job is to create the conditions where they might find it."

Lena felt herself leaning forward, drawn in by Echo's presence. "And do they? Find what they're looking for?"

"Some do," Echo replied, her gaze still fixed on the pulsing life below. "Others discover they were looking for the wrong thing entirely." She turned back to Lena, her eyes holding a depth that made Lena's breath catch. "But that's the beauty of a space like this—it allows for both recognition and revelation."

Echo shifted slightly, her dress rippling like liquid metal in the low light. "I believe in creating environments where people feel safe enough to be authentic. Where the masks we all wear can be set aside, even if just for a night." Her hand gestured toward the crowd below, the movement elegant and precise. "Look how they move together, how they orbit each other. Each seeking their own constellation to belong to."

Lena followed her gaze, seeing the club with new eyes. What had seemed like a mosaic now, each person a unique tile contributing to the whole. The patterns of movement, the clusters that formed and dissolved, the electric moments when strangers connected—it all seemed orchestrated, yet organic.

"My greatest joy," Echo continued, her voice softening further, "is creating a space where everyone feels they belong." She gestured toward a shy-looking woman at the bar who was being gently drawn into conversation by a regular. "Where the lonely find community, where the misunderstood find acceptance."

Lena watched as the woman's face transformed, tension melting into a tentative smile. The simple human connection unfolding below suddenly seemed profound—a small miracle happening under Echo's watchful eye.

"I believe in the power of sanctuary," Echo said. "A place where people can exhale the breath they've been holding all day, sometimes all their lives." Her hand moved in a graceful arc, encompassing the entire club. "A home for those who haven't found one elsewhere."

The sincerity in Echo's voice touched something in Lena—a recognition of her own wandering, her own search for belonging that she channeled into constant movement rather than confronting directly.

"The Glass Heel and The Heel's Nest are two halves

of the same heart," Echo continued, her gaze returning to the dance floor where bodies had begun to move with greater abandon as Heather's beat deepened. "Down here, people discover their desires in the open. Upstairs, they explore them in private. The two are inseparable—one breathes life into the other."

Lena felt the truth of Echo's words resonating through her like the bass notes from below. Not as intellectual understanding, but as something visceral and immediate. The club wasn't just a nightlife venue; the hotel wasn't just accommodation. Together, they formed an ecosystem of human connection, of self-discovery that began in public and culminated in private.

"Is that why the rooms upstairs are all so different?" Lena asked, leaning closer to be heard over the music that had swelled in volume. "To accommodate different desires?"

Echo nodded, a knowing smile playing at the corners of her mouth. "Each room is a canvas for a different fantasy, a different need." Her fingers traced an invisible pattern on the velvet upholstery between them. "Some guests come seeking passion, others tenderness. Some want to surrender control, others to claim it."

Adrian shifted beside Lena, his thigh pressing against hers. The contact sent a current of warmth up her leg.

"The most powerful desires are often the ones we struggle to name," Echo continued, her near-silver eyes holding Lena's with unexpected intensity. "My job—our job—is to create spaces where those desires can be safely recognized, spoken, explored."

Lena thought of the fourth floor with its crimson lighting and mysterious doorways. "And the most sacred desires get the most private spaces," she murmured.

Echo's smile deepened, approval flickering in her eyes. "You understand."

The music shifted, Heather's skillful hands guiding the tempo into something slower, more sensual. The energy on the dance floor transformed, couples drawing closer, singles pairing off with meaningful glances.

Adrian's fingers brushed against Lena's wrist, the touch light but deliberate. "Dance with me?" he asked, rising to his feet and offering his hand.

Her heart skipped as she placed her palm against his. The warmth of his skin sent a current up her arm, familiar now but no less potent. Echo watched them with knowing eyes as Adrian led Lena toward the stairs, his fingers intertwined with hers.

"Enjoy your evening," Echo called after them, her melodic voice carrying over the music. "Some moments are meant to be treasured."

The words followed Lena down the spiral staircase, settling into her chest like a stone dropped into still water. Treasured. Because this was their last night. Tomorrow she'd board a plane and leave this sanctuary behind.

The dance floor had grown crowded, bodies moving in hypnotic synchronicity to Heather's steady beat. Adrian guided Lena through the press of people with gentle pressure at the small of her back. The crowd seemed to part for them, opening a space near the center where colored lights swirled in patterns across the polished wood.

Adrian turned to face her, his eyes catching fragments of blue and purple from the lights overhead. His hand settled at her waist, warm and sure through the thin fabric of her dress. Lena stepped closer, her body remembering the shape of his from nights before. Her palm found his shoulder, feeling the solid strength beneath expensive wool.

The music pulsed around them, a heartbeat made audible. Adrian began to move, guiding her with subtle pressure into a slow sway that matched the rhythm perfectly. Their bodies found harmony without effort, as if they'd been dancing together for years rather than days.

Lena's gaze locked with his, the connection between them deepening with each measure of music. The room around them blurred into insignificance—the other dancers, the shifting lights, even the passage of time itself faded until there was only Adrian, only this moment suspended between one heartbeat and the next.

His hand at her waist drew her closer until the space between them vanished. Heat bloomed where their bodies touched—chest to chest, thigh against thigh. Lena could feel his heartbeat against her own, the steady rhythm slightly faster than the music they moved to.

"I keep thinking about tomorrow," she whispered, the words meant only for him despite the noise surrounding them.

Adrian's fingers tightened slightly at her waist. "Don't," he murmured, his breath warm against her temple. "Just be here with me now."

Lena nodded, letting her cheek rest against his shoulder. The subtle scent of his cologne mingled with something warmer, more personal—a scent that was uniquely his. She closed her eyes, surrendering to the moment, to the sensation of being held—truly held—by someone who saw her, all of her.

The music swelled around them, Heather's masterful hands guiding the crowd through waves of rhythm. Each song melted seamlessly into the next, time becoming fluid, measured only by the steady beat and the synchronized movement of bodies.

Lena lost herself in the dance, in the hypnotic sway of their bodies moving as one. Adrian's hand at the small of her back felt like an anchor, keeping her tethered to this moment when everything else threatened to slip away. The colored lights painted his features in ever-changing hues—now blue, now purple, now a deep crimson that made his eyes look almost black.

As the night deepened, the club grew more crowded, the energy building like a tide. Lena barely noticed the press of bodies around them, focused entirely on the man before her, on memorizing every detail—the exact curve of his smile, the tiny scar near his temple, the way his eyes crinkled at the corners when he looked at her.

From above, Echo watched them with knowing eyes, her silver dress catching fragments of light as she leaned against the railing of her private booth. When Adrian's gaze briefly met hers, she offered a subtle nod, an acknowledgment of something precious unfolding on her dance floor.

The music shifted again, the tempo slowing further as Heather guided the room into something deeper, more sensual. Adrian drew Lena closer, if that was even possible, his arm encircling her waist completely. Her hand slid from his shoulder to the nape of his neck, fingers threading through the soft hair there.

"I want to remember this," she whispered against his collar, her words nearly lost in the music.

Adrian's lips brushed her temple, not quite a kiss but an intimate touch that sent warmth cascading down her spine. "So do I," he murmured, his voice a vibration she felt more than heard.

They moved together with unhurried grace, each step deliberate, as if they were imprinting this dance into their muscles, their bones. There was no showing off, no elaborate movements—just the slow, synchronized sway of two bodies that had learned each other's rhythms.

Lena's dress whispered against Adrian's suit as they turned, the fabric creating a soft friction between them. His hand splayed wider at her back, drawing her impossibly closer until she could feel his heartbeat against her chest, strong and steady and slightly faster than the music.

"You're beautiful," he said, his lips close to her ear. "In this light, in any light."

The simple words warmed her from within, spreading outward until she felt luminous, as if she might glow in the darkness of the club. She tipped her face up to his, their eyes meeting in a gaze so intimate it felt like another form of touch.

Around them, the club seemed to fade into a muted backdrop of color and sound. The music deepened, slowing to a rhythm that matched the beating of their hearts. Adrian's hand slid to the small of her back, drawing her closer until no space remained between them. His eyes never left hers as they moved together, their bodies remembering each other with every step.

Lena traced the curve of his shoulder with her fingertips, committing the solid warmth of him to memory. The scent of his cologne mingled with the faint salt of his skin, a combination she knew she would search for in crowds long after tonight. His breath brushed against her temple, sending tendrils of warmth down her spine.

"I wish we could stay like this," she whispered, her words meant only for him.

Adrian's fingers tightened slightly at her waist. He didn't answer with words, but the gentle pressure of his touch spoke volumes. They both knew the impossibility of her wish, which made holding onto this moment all the more precious.

The colored lights swept across them in slow waves—amber, then blue, then violet—painting their skin in ephemeral hues that appeared and vanished like fleeting possibilities. Each step they took felt weighted with significance, as if the dance floor had become an altar where they offered up this final shared moment.

Lena rested her cheek against his chest, closing her eyes to better absorb the sensation of being held by him. The steady thrum of his heartbeat beneath her ear became its own kind of music, one she tried to memorize beneath the club's melodic pulse. His chin settled lightly atop her head, completing the circle of their embrace.

They moved in perfect synchronicity, turning slowly in place as the song unfurled around them. No elaborate steps, no flourishes—just the gentle sway of two people holding tight to something already slipping away.

When the final notes of the song faded into silence, neither moved immediately. They remained locked together in the moment after music, suspended in the fragile space between what was and what would be. Lena felt Adrian's chest rise and fall with a deep breath before he finally loosened his hold, just enough to look down at her.

His eyes held a question she couldn't answer. Instead, she took his hand, lacing her fingers through his. Without words, they turned from the dance floor, slipping between other couples toward the stairs.

The journey back to her room passed in meaningful silence. Each step up the staircase felt like both an ending and a beginning—moving away from the shared magic of the club while drawing closer to the privacy that awaited them. Adrian's hand remained firmly clasped in hers, his thumb occasionally brushing across her knuckles in a gesture that sent small shivers up her arm.

They walked in silence down the third-floor hallway, their shoes sinking into carpet thick enough to swallow sound. Outside Room 312, Lena's fingers trembled slightly against the brass key. Tomorrow loomed in her mind, making the air feel suddenly too thin to breathe properly. The door swung open, then shut behind them with a decisive click that sealed them away from the world. Inside, the club's bass became just a faint pulse beneath their feet—a reminder of what they'd left behind. As Lena turned the deadbolt, the lock's mechanism slid into place with a sound that seemed to say: here, now, there is only truth.

When she faced Adrian again, something had shifted in his eyes—a vulnerability that made her chest tighten. He stood perfectly still in the center of the room, waiting. For her. The realization washed over Lena like warm water.

She moved toward him slowly, her fingers finding the knot of his tie. The silk was smooth beneath her touch as she loosened it with deliberate care, sliding it free from his collar in one fluid motion. Adrian's breath caught as she undid the first button of his shirt, then the second, her knuckles brushing against the warm skin beneath.

"Let me," he whispered, reaching for the zipper at the back of her dress. His fingers were steady but unhurried, each movement infused with a reverence that made her skin prickle with awareness. The zipper's descent was nearly silent, a whispered secret between them as the burgundy fabric loosened its hold on her body.

Adrian's hands slid beneath the open back of her dress, palms warm against her skin as he eased the garment from her shoulders. It fell in a ripple of fabric, pooling at her feet like spilled wine. His gaze traveled over her with such focused attention that Lena felt it like a physical caress, raising goosebumps along her arms, her stomach, her thighs.

She returned to the buttons of his shirt, working her way down with meticulous care. Each newly revealed inch of skin became a canvas for her fingertips to explore—the hollow at the base of his throat, the defined curve of his collarbone, the subtle ridges of his ribs. When she pushed the shirt from his shoulders, Adrian shrugged out of it with fluid grace, letting it join her dress on the floor.

Their disrobing continued in this ceremonial fashion—each garment removed with deliberate tenderness, each newly exposed expanse of skin honored with touch. Adrian knelt to slip off her heels, his hands cradling her calf with gentle pressure as he freed first one foot, then the other. When he rose, his hands traced the length of her legs, mapping the curve of her calves, the sensitive hollow behind her knees, the soft swell of her thighs.

Lena worked the buckle of his belt, the leather sliding through the loops with a soft hiss that seemed loud in the quiet room. His trousers followed, the expensive wool falling away to reveal strong thighs and the evident desire straining against black boxer briefs. Her fingers hooked into the elastic waistband, easing them down with the same unhurried care he had shown her.

When they stood before each other, fully revealed, Adrian's hands framed her face with a tenderness that made her breath catch. His touch was feather-light, fingers tracing the curve of her cheekbone, the line of her jaw, as if committing every contour to memory. Lena leaned into his palm, her eyes holding his in the soft lamplight.

They moved to the bed in wordless agreement, the sheets cool against their skin as they sank down together. Adrian hovered above her, his weight supported on his forearms, creating a shelter of warmth and shadow. His eyes never left hers as he lowered his head, brushing his lips against her forehead, her temples, the tip of her nose—each kiss a benediction.

Lena's hands mapped the landscape of his back, feeling the subtle shift of muscle beneath smooth skin. She traced the bumps of his spine, one by one, as if counting treasures. When her fingertips reached the nape of his neck, she drew him down to her, their lips meeting in a kiss that held none of the urgency of previous nights. Instead, it unfolded with deliberate slowness, a shared breath that deepened by degrees.

The world beyond their joined bodies ceased to exist. Time stretched and slowed, measured only by heartbeats and shared breaths. Adrian's hands moved over her with reverent precision, rediscovering places they had explored before, but with new attention—the sensitive hollow of her throat, the curve where her waist flared to hip, the soft underside of her breast.

Lena arched into his touch, her body remembering his with a certainty that belied their brief time together. Her fingers tangled in his hair, drawing his mouth to the pulse point at her neck. His breath was warm against her skin, raising goosebumps that spread like ripples across still water.

When he entered her from behind, his chest pressed warm against the curve of her spine, it was with such careful tenderness that tears pricked behind her closed eyelids. Their bodies joined with familiar ease, finding a rhythm as natural as breathing. Lena turned her head to find Adrian watching her over her shoulder, his gaze so intense that something caught in her chest—a recognition that transcended the physical connection they shared.

They moved together without hurry, each undulation of their joined bodies a language spoken without words. Her hands found his shoulders, feeling the controlled strength there as he supported his weight above her. His fingers interlaced with hers, palms pressing together in a gesture as intimate as their bodies' connection.

The pleasure built slowly, a warmth that spread from where they were joined through her entire body. Lena watched Adrian's face transform as they moved together, memorizing the way his eyelids fluttered when she shifted beneath him, the way his lips parted on a silent exhale when she tightened around him.

Adrian's name fell from her lips like a prayer as the tension coiled tighter within her. She felt the solid warmth of his chest against her back, his breath stirring the fine hairs at her nape as he moved deeper inside her from behind. His arm wrapped around her waist, drawing her closer until their bodies formed a perfect curve, heartbeats synchronizing through the press of skin against skin.

The crescendo built with exquisite slowness, each wave of pleasure more intense than the last until Lena felt herself balancing on the edge of oblivion. Adrian's lips traced the sensitive curve where her shoulder met her neck, his eyes finding hers as she turned her head toward him. He held her gaze in the dim light, refusing to let her look away as the tension finally broke. She cried out softly, her body trembling from crown to toe against his as ecstasy washed through her in pulsing waves that contracted every muscle. Adrian followed moments later, his forehead pressed against her shoulder blade, breath hot against her skin as he shuddered and released deeply inside her, the heat of his climax intensifying the lingering pulses of her own.

They remained joined afterward, Adrian's chest still pressed against the curve of her back, neither willing to break the connection. His weight settled half beside, half atop her, his heartbeat gradually slowing against her shoulder blade. Lena's fingers found his hand at her hip, tracing the knuckles, memorizing the texture of his skin as her body continued to hold him inside her from behind.

When he finally slipped free and shifted to lie beside her, his arm remained draped across her waist, keeping her close. The sheets tangled around their legs, still warm from their shared heat. Lena turned to face him, her head finding the perfect hollow between his shoulder and chest. His heartbeat echoed beneath her ear, a steady rhythm that pulled her toward sleep.

Outside, the last snowflakes drifted past their window, illuminated by the amber glow of streetlights. The city lay silent beneath its white blanket, traffic muted, footsteps absorbed by the snow. Tomorrow would bring noise and movement again—plows scraping streets clean, people emerging from shelter, planes rising into the sky. But for now, the world held its breath, giving them this one last pocket of stillness.

Adrian's breathing deepened, his chest rising and falling in the slow rhythm of approaching sleep. His fingers traced one final path along her arm before stilling, resting against the curve of her elbow. Lena fought against her heavy eyelids, trying to commit every sensation to memory—the warmth of his skin against hers, the subtle scent that was uniquely his, the perfect weight of his arm across her body.

Sleep claimed her despite her resistance, drawing her down into darkness wrapped in his embrace. Their limbs remained entangled, as if even unconsciousness couldn't persuade them to let go. The snow continued its silent fall outside, cocooning their room in a hushed, white world where nothing existed beyond the two of them.

Lena woke first, dawn's gray light filtering through the partially drawn curtains. For a moment, she remained perfectly still, absorbing the sensation of Adrian's body curved around hers, his arm heavy across her waist, his breath warm against the nape of her neck. She studied the aftermath of yesterday's storm through the window. The snow had stopped falling sometime before noon the day before, leaving the world crystallized and still. Now the city was waking up beneath its day-old white blanket, the pristine surface already marred by plows that had carved dark, practical channels through the streets below.

Her flight would leave in four hours.

Lena carefully disentangled herself from Adrian's

embrace, holding her breath as he stirred slightly before settling back into deep sleep. She sat at the edge of the bed, allowing herself one long moment to study him—the fan of dark lashes against his cheeks, the slight furrow between his brows, the curve of his lips that had traced every inch of her skin. In sleep, his face held a vulnerability that made her heart ache with a feeling too raw to name.

She dressed quietly in the half-light, pulling on jeans and a soft sweater, movements deliberate to avoid waking him. Her suitcase waited by the door, already packed except for her toiletries. She gathered these with practiced efficiency, the routine of departure familiar after years of constant motion.

At the desk, she paused, pulling out the hotel stationery and a pen. Words had always come easily to her—it was her profession, after all—but now they stuck in her throat, resisting being committed to paper. What could she possibly say that would encompass all that had happened between them? How could she distill this weekend into a note that wouldn't sound trite or, worse, dismissive?

She wrote and discarded three versions before settling on the simplest truth. Folding her business card inside the note, she placed it on the nightstand where he would see it immediately upon waking. The message was brief but certain: You're more than a weekend story.

Lena stood in the doorway for one last moment, watching the rise and fall of Adrian's chest beneath the sheets. The urge to climb back into bed, to curl against his warmth and pretend morning hadn't come, was almost overwhelming. Instead, she silently closed the door behind her.

The lobby was empty save for the night manager, who nodded sleepily as Lena signed her checkout forms. Outside, the air bit at her cheeks, sharp and clean after days of snowbound stillness. She paused on the threshold, adjusting Adrian's scarf around her neck. She'd meant to leave it, but at the last moment, she couldn't bear to part with this small piece of him.

The cashmere slipped against her skin like a memory, carrying his scent—cedar and coffee and something uniquely him that made her chest tighten. She wound it more securely, tucking the ends inside her coat, knowing she'd keep it folded in tissue paper in her bedside drawer back home, taking it out on nights when the space beside her felt too empty, pressing it to her face to recapture this moment, this place, this man.

More from The Glass Heel Series
by Tatiana Vixen Reyes

First Step
A single step into The Glass Heel becomes the beginning
of a journey she can never walk back.

Room 312
Behind the door of Room 312, she discovers the kind of
connection that only exists when the world is shut out.

Neon Diner
At the Neon Diner, between coffee and confession, she
discovers exactly what she's been starving for.

Sanctuary Nights
In the hush of Sanctuary Nights, she finds the safety that
finally lets her let go.